Evan Harrington

Volume 2

by

George Meredith

Double 9 BOOKS

Evan Harrington
Volume 2

by George Meredith

ISBN: 978-93-63053-33-5

Published by

DOUBLE 9 BOOKS
2/13-B, Ansari Road
Daryaganj, New Delhi – 110002
info@double9books.com
www.double9books.com
Tel. 011-40042856

CONTENTS

CHAPTER VIII
INTRODUCES AN ECCENTRIC

At the Aurora—one of those rare antiquated taverns, smelling of comfortable time and solid English fare, that had sprung up in the great coffee days, when taverns were clubs, and had since subsisted on the attachment of steady bachelor Templars there had been dismay, and even sorrow, for a month. The most constant patron of the establishment—an old gentleman who had dined there for seven-and-twenty years, four days in the week, off dishes dedicated to the particular days, and had grown grey with the landlady, the cook, and the head-waiter—this old gentleman had abruptly withheld his presence. Though his name, his residence, his occupation, were things only to be speculated on at the Aurora, he was very well known there, and as men are best to be known: that is to say, by their habits. Some affection for him also was felt. The landlady looked on him as a part of the house. The cook and the waiter were accustomed to receive acceptable compliments from him monthly. His precise words, his regular ancient jokes, his pint of Madeira and after-pint of Port, his antique bow to the landlady, passing out and in, his method of spreading his table-napkin on his lap and looking up at the ceiling ere he fell to, and how he talked to himself during the repast, and indulged in short chuckles, and the one look of perfect felicity that played over his features when he had taken his first sip of Port—these were matters it pained them at the Aurora to have to remember.

For three weeks the resolution not to regard him as of the past was general. The Aurora was the old gentleman's home. Men do not play truant from home at sixty years of age. He must, therefore, be seriously indisposed. The kind heart of the landlady fretted to think he might have no soul to nurse and care for him; but she kept his corner near the fire-place vacant, and took care that his pint of Madeira was there. The belief was gaining ground that he had gone, and that nothing but his ghost would ever sit there again. Still the melancholy ceremony continued: for the landlady was not without a secret hope, that in spite of his reserve and the mystery surrounding him, he would have sent her a last word. The cook and head-waiter, interrogated as to their dealings with the old gentleman, testified solemnly to the fact of their having performed their duty by him. They would not go against their interests so much as to forget one of his ways, they said—taking oath, as it were, by their lower nature, in order to be credited: an instinct men have of one another. The landlady could not contradict them, for the old gentleman had made no complaint; but then she called to memory that fifteen years back, in such and such a year, Wednesday's dish had been, by shameful oversight, furnished him for Tuesday's, and he had eaten it quietly, but refused his Port; which pathetic event had caused alarm and inquiry, when the error was discovered, and apologized for, the old gentleman merely saying, "Don't let it happen again." Next day he drank his Port, as usual, and the wheels of the Aurora went smoothly. The landlady was thus justified in averring that something had been done by somebody, albeit unable to point to anything specific. Women, who are almost as deeply bound to habit as old gentlemen, possess more of its spiritual element, and are warned by dreams, omens, creepings of the flesh, unwonted chills, suicide of china, and other shadowing signs, when a break is to be anticipated, or, has occurred. The landlady of the Aurora tavern was visited by none of these, and with that beautiful trust which habit gives, and which boastful love or vainer earthly qualities would fail in effecting, she ordered that the pint of Madeira should stand from six o'clock in the evening till seven—a small monument of confidence in him who was at one instant the "poor old dear"; at another, the "naughty old gad-about"; further, the "faithless old-good-for-nothing"; and again, the "blessed pet" of the landlady's parlour, alternately and indiscriminately apostrophized by herself, her sister, and daughter.

On the last day of the month a step was heard coming up the long alley which led from the riotous scrambling street to the plentiful cheerful heart of the Aurora. The landlady knew the step. She checked the natural flutterings of her ribbons, toned down the strong simper that was on her lips, rose, pushed aside her daughter, and, as the step approached, curtsied composedly. Old Habit lifted his hat, and passed. With the same touching confidence in the Aurora that the Aurora had in him, he went straight to his corner, expressed no surprise at his welcome by the Madeira, and thereby apparently indicated that his appearance should enjoy a similar immunity.

As of old, he called "Jonathan!" and was not to be disturbed till he did so. Seeing that Jonathan smirked and twiddled his napkin, the old gentleman added, "Thursday!"

But Jonathan, a man, had not his mistress's keen intuition of the deportment necessitated by the case, or was incapable of putting the screw upon weak excited nature, for he continued to smirk, and was remarking how glad he was, he was sure, and something he had dared to think and almost to fear, when the old gentleman called to him, as if he were at the other end of the room, "Will you order Thursday, or not, sir?" Whereat Jonathan flew, and two or three cosy diners glanced up from their plates, or the paper, smiled, and pursued their capital occupation.

"Glad to see me!" the old gentleman muttered, querulously. "Of course, glad to see a customer! Why do you tell me that? Talk! tattle! might as well have a woman to wait—just!"

He wiped his forehead largely with his handkerchief; as one whom Calamity hunted a little too hard in summer weather.

"No tumbling-room for the wine, too!"

That was his next grievance. He changed the pint of Madeira from his left side to his right, and went under his handkerchief again, feverishly. The world was severe with this old gentleman.

"Ah! clock wrong now!"

He leaned back like a man who can no longer carry his burdens, informing Jonathan, on his coming up to place the roll of bread and firm butter, that he was forty seconds too fast, as if it were a capital offence, and he deserved to step into Eternity for outstripping Time.

"But, I daresay, you don't understand the importance of a minute," said the old gentleman, bitterly. "Not you, or any of you. Better if we had run a little ahead of your minute, perhaps—and the rest of you! Do you think you can cancel the mischief that's done in the world in that minute, sir, by hurrying ahead like that? Tell me!"

Rather at a loss, Jonathan scanned the clock seriously, and observed that it was not quite a minute too fast.

The old gentleman pulled out his watch. He grunted that a lying clock was hateful to him; subsequently sinking into contemplation of his thumbs,—a sign known to Jonathan as indicative of the old gentleman's system having resolved, in spite of external outrages, to be fortified with calm to meet the repast.

It is not fair to go behind an eccentric; but the fact was, this old gentleman was slightly ashamed of his month's vagrancy and cruel conduct, and cloaked his behaviour toward the Aurora, in all the charges he could muster against it. He was very human, albeit an odd form of the race.

Happily for his digestion of Thursday, the cook, warned by Jonathan, kept the old gentleman's time, not the Aurora's: and the dinner was correct; the dinner was eaten in peace; he began to address his plate vigorously, poured out his Madeira, and chuckled, as the familiar ideas engendered by good wine were revived in him. Jonathan reported at the bar that the old gentleman was all right again.

One would like here to pause, while our worthy ancient feeds, and indulge in a short essay on Habit, to show what a sacred and admirable thing it is that makes flimsy Time substantial, and consolidates his triple life. It is proof that we have come to the end of dreams and Time's delusions, and are determined to sit down at Life's feast and carve for ourselves. Its day is the child of yesterday, and has a claim on to-morrow. Whereas those who have no such plan of existence and sum of their wisdom to show, the winds blow them as they list. Consider, then, mercifully the wrath of him on whom carelessness or forgetfulness has brought a snap in the links of Habit. You incline to scorn him because, his slippers misplaced, or asparagus not on his table the first day of a particular Spring month, he gazes blankly and sighs as one who saw the End. To you it may appear small. You call to him to be a man. He is: but he is also an immortal, and his confidence in unceasing orderly progression is rudely dashed.

But the old gentleman has finished his dinner and his Madeira, and says: "Now, Jonathan, 'thock' the Port!"—his joke when matters have gone well: meant to express the sound of the uncorking, probably. The habit of making good jokes is rare, as you know: old gentlemen have not yet attained to it: nevertheless Jonathan enjoys this one, which has seen a generation in and out, for he knows its purport to be, "My heart is open."

And now is a great time with this old gentleman. He sips, and in his eyes the world grows rosy, and he exchanges mute or monosyllable salutes here and there. His habit is to avoid converse; but he will let a light remark season meditation.

He says to Jonathan: "The bill for the month."

"Yes, sir," Jonathan replies. "Would you not prefer, sir, to have the items added on to the month ensuing?"

"I asked you for the bill of the month," said the old gentleman, with an irritated voice and a twinkle in his eye.

Jonathan bowed; but his aspect betrayed perplexity, and that perplexity was soon shared by the landlady for Jonathan said, he was convinced the old gentleman intended to pay for sixteen days, and the landlady could not bring her hand to charge him for more than two. Here was the dilemma foreseen by the old gentleman, and it added vastly to the flavour of the Port.

Pleasantly tickled, he sat gazing at his glass, and let the minutes fly. He knew the part he would act in his little farce. If charged for the whole month, he would peruse the bill deliberately, and perhaps cry out "Hulloa?"

and then snap at Jonathan for the interposition of a remark. But if charged for two days, he would wish to be told whether they were demented, those people outside, and scornfully return the bill to Jonathan.

A slap on the shoulder, and a voice: "Found you at last, Tom!" violently shattered the excellent plot, and made the old gentleman start. He beheld Mr. Andrew Cogglesby.

"Drinking Port, Tom?" said Mr. Andrew. "I'll join you": and he sat down opposite to him, rubbing his hands and pushing back his hair.

Jonathan entering briskly with the bill, fell back a step, in alarm. The old gentleman, whose inviolacy was thus rudely assailed, sat staring at the intruder, his mouth compressed, and three fingers round his glass, which it was doubtful whether he was not going to hurl at him.

"Waiter!" Mr. Andrew carelessly hailed, "a pint of this Port, if you please."

Jonathan sought the countenance of the old gentleman.

"Do you hear, sir?" cried the latter, turning his wrath on him. "Another pint!" He added: "Take back the bill"; and away went Jonathan to relate fresh marvels to his mistress.

Mr. Andrew then addressed the old gentleman in the most audacious manner.

"Astonished to see me here, Tom? Dare say you are. I knew you came somewhere in this neighbourhood, and, as I wanted to speak to you very particularly, and you wouldn't be visible till Monday, why, I spied into two or three places, and here I am."

You might see they were brothers. They had the same bushy eyebrows, the same healthy colour in their cheeks, the same thick shoulders, and brisk way of speaking, and clear, sharp, though kindly, eyes; only Tom was cast in larger proportions than Andrew, and had gotten the grey furniture of Time for his natural wear. Perhaps, too, a cross in early life had a little twisted him, and set his mouth in a rueful bunch, out of which occasionally came biting things. Mr. Andrew carried his head up, and eyed every man living with the benevolence of a patriarch, dashed with the impudence of a London sparrow. Tom had a nagging air, and a trifle of acridity on his broad features. Still, any one at a glance could have sworn they were brothers, and Jonathan unhesitatingly proclaimed it at the Aurora bar.

Mr. Andrew's hands were working together, and at them, and at his face, the old gentleman continued to look with a firmly interrogating air.

"Want to know what brings me, Tom? I'll tell you presently. Hot,—isn't it?"

"What the deuce are you taking exercise for?" the old gentleman burst out, and having unlocked his mouth, he began to puff and alter his posture.

"There you are, thawed in a minute!" said Mr. Andrew. "What's an eccentric? a child grown grey. It isn't mine; I read it somewhere. Ah, here's the Port! good, I'll warrant."

Jonathan deferentially uncorked, excessive composure on his visage. He arranged the table-cloth to a nicety, fixed the bottle with exactness, and was only sent scudding by the old gentleman's muttering of: "Eavesdropping pie!" followed by a short, "Go!" and even then he must delay to sweep off a particular crumb.

"Good it is!" said Mr. Andrew, rolling the flavour on his lips, as he put down his glass. "I follow you in Port, Tom. Elder brother!"

The old gentleman also drank, and was mollified enough to reply: "Shan't follow you in Parliament."

"Haven't forgiven that yet, Tom?"

"No great harm done when you're silent."

"Capital Port!" said Mr. Andrew, replenishing the glasses. "I ought to have inquired where they kept the best Port. I might have known you'd stick by it. By the way, talking of Parliament, there's talk of a new election for Fallowfield. You have a vote there. Will you give it to Jocelyn? There's talk of his standing.

"If he'll wear petticoats, I'll give him my vote."

"There you go, Tom!"

"I hate masquerades. You're penny trumpets of the women. That tattle comes from the bed-curtains. When a petticoat steps forward I give it my vote, or else I button it up in my pocket."

This was probably one of the longest speeches he had ever delivered at the Aurora. There was extra Port in it. Jonathan, who from his place of observation noted the length of time it occupied, though he was unable to gather the context, glanced at Mr. Andrew with a sly satisfaction. Mr. Andrew, laughing, signalled for another pint.

"So you've come here for my vote, have you?" said Mr. Tom.

"Why, no; not exactly that," Mr. Andrew answered, blinking and passing it by.

Jonathan brought the fresh pint, and Tom filled for himself, drank, and said emphatically, and with a confounding voice:

"Your women have been setting you on me, sir!"

Andrew protested that he was entirely mistaken.

"You're the puppet of your women!"

"Well, Tom, not in this instance. Here's to the bachelors, and brother Tom at their head!"

It seemed to be Andrew's object to help his companion to carry a certain quantity of Port, as if he knew a virtue it had to subdue him, and to have fixed on a particular measure that he should hold before he addressed him specially. Arrived at this, he said:

"Look here, Tom. I know your ways. I shouldn't have bothered you here; I never have before; but we couldn't very well talk it over in business hours; and besides you're never at the Brewery till Monday, and the matter's rather urgent."

"Why don't you speak like that in Parliament?" the old man interposed.

"Because Parliament isn't my brother," replied Mr. Andrew. "You know, Tom, you never quite took to my wife's family."

"I'm not a match for fine ladies, Nan."

"Well, Harriet would have taken to you, Tom, and will now, if you'll let her. Of course, it's a pity if she's ashamed of—hem! You found it out about the Lymport people, Tom, and, you've kept the secret and respected her feelings, and I thank you for it. Women are odd in those things, you know. She mustn't imagine I've heard a whisper. I believe it would kill her."

The old gentleman shook silently.

"Do you want me to travel over the kingdom, hawking her for the daughter of a marquis?"

"Now, don't joke, Tom. I'm serious. Are you not a Radical at heart? Why do you make such a set against the poor women? What do we spring from?"

"I take off my hat, Nan, when I see a cobbler's stall."

"And I, Tom, don't care a rush who knows it. Homo—something; but we never had much schooling. We've thriven, and should help those we can. We've got on in the world..."

"Wife come back from Lymport?" sneered Tom.

Andrew hurriedly, and with some confusion, explained that she had not been able to go, on account of the child.

"Account of the child!" his brother repeated, working his chin contemptuously. "Sisters gone?"

"They're stopping with us," said Andrew, reddening.

"So the tailor was left to the kites and the crows. Ah! hum!" and Tom chuckled.

"You're angry with me, Tom, for coming here," said Andrew. "I see what it is. Thought how it would be! You're offended, old Tom."

"Come where you like," returned Tom, "the place is open. It's a fool that hopes for peace anywhere. They sent a woman here to wait on me, this day month."

"That's a shame!" said Mr. Andrew, propitiatingly. "Well, never mind, Tom: the women are sometimes in the way.—Evan went down to bury his father. He's there now. You wouldn't see him when he was at the Brewery, Tom. He's—upon my honour! he's a good young fellow."

"A fine young gentleman, I've no doubt, Nan."

"A really good lad, Tom. No nonsense. I've come here to speak to you about him."

Mr. Andrew drew a letter from his pocket, pursuing: "Just throw aside your prejudices, and read this. It's a letter I had from him this morning. But first I must tell you how the case stands."

"Know more than you can tell me, Nan," said Tom, turning over the flavour of a gulp of his wine.

"Well, then, just let me repeat it. He has been capitally educated; he has always been used to good society: well, we mustn't sneer at it: good society's better than bad, you'll allow. He has refined tastes: well, you wouldn't like to live among crossing-sweepers, Tom. He's clever and accomplished, can speak and write in three languages: I wish I had his abilities. He has good manners: well, Tom, you know you like them as well as anybody. And now—but read for yourself."

"Yah!" went old Tom. "The women have been playing the fool with him since he was a baby. I read his rigmarole? No."

Mr. Andrew shrugged his shoulders, and opened the letter, saying: "Well, listen"; and then he coughed, and rapidly skimmed the introductory part. "Excuses himself for addressing me formally—poor boy! Circumstances have altered his position towards the world: found his father's affairs in a bad state: only chance of paying off father's debts to undertake management of business, and bind himself to so much a year. But there, Tom, if you won't read it, you miss the poor young fellow's character. He says that he has forgotten his station: fancied he was superior to trade, but hates debt; and will not allow anybody to throw dirt at his father's name, while he can work to clear it; and will sacrifice his pride. Come, Tom, that's manly, isn't it? I call it touching, poor lad!"

Manly it may have been, but the touching part of it was a feature missed in Mr. Andrew's hands. At any rate, it did not appear favourably to impress Tom, whose chin had gathered its ominous puckers, as he inquired:

"What's the trade? he don't say."

Andrew added, with a wave of the hand: "Out of a sort of feeling for his sisters—I like him for it. Now what I want to ask you, Tom, is, whether we can't assist him in some way! Why couldn't we take him into our office, and fix him there, eh? If he works well—we're both getting old, and my brats are chicks—we might, by-and-by, give him a share."

"Make a brewer of him? Ha! there'd be another mighty sacrifice for his pride!"

"Come, come, Tom," said Andrew, "he's my wife's brother, and I'm yours; and—there, you know what women are. They like to preserve appearances: we ought to consider them."

"Preserve appearances!" echoed Tom: "ha! who'll do that for them better than a tailor?"

Andrew was an impatient little man, fitter for a kind action than to plead a cause. Jeering jarred on him; and from the moment his brother began it, he was of small service to Evan. He flung back against the partition of the compound, rattling it to the disturbance of many a quiet digestion.

"Tom," he cried, "I believe you're a screw!"

"Never said I wasn't," rejoined Tom, as he finished his glass. "I'm a bachelor, and a person—you're married, and an object. I won't have the tailor's family at my coat-tails."

Do you mean to say, Tom, you don't like the young fellow? The Countess says he's half engaged to an heiress; and he has a chance of appointments—of course, nothing may come of them. But do you mean to say, you don't like him for what he has done?"

Tom made his jaw disagreeably prominent. "'Fraid I'm guilty of that crime."

"And you that swear at people pretending to be above their station!" exclaimed Andrew. "I shall get in a passion. I can't stand this. Here, waiter! what have I to pay?"

"Go," cried the time-honoured guest of the Aurora to Jonathan advancing.

Andrew pressed the very roots of his hair back from his red forehead, and sat upright and resolute, glancing at Tom. And now ensued a curious scene of family blood. For no sooner did elderly Tom observe this bantam-like demeanour of his brother, than he ruffled his feathers likewise, and looked down on him, agitating his wig over a prodigious frown. Whereof came the following sharp colloquy; Andrew beginning:

"I'll pay off the debts out of my own pocket."

"You can make a greater fool of yourself, then?"

"He shan't be a tailor!"

"He shan't be a brewer!"

"I say he shall live like a gentleman!"

"I say he shall squat like a Turk!"

Bang went Andrew's hand on the table: "I've pledged my word, mind!"

Tom made a counter demonstration: "And I'll have my way!"

"Hang it! I can be as eccentric as you," said Andrew.

"And I as much a donkey as you, if I try hard," said Tom.

Something of the cobbler's stall followed this; till waxing furious, Tom sung out to Jonathan, hovering around them in watchful timidity, "More Port!" and the words immediately fell oily on the wrath of the brothers; both commenced wiping their heads with their handkerchiefs the faces of both emerged and met, with a half-laugh: and, severally determined to keep to what they had spoken, there was a tacit accord between them to drop the subject.

Like sunshine after smart rain, the Port shone on these brothers. Like a voice from the pastures after the bellowing of the thunder, Andrew's voice asked: "Got rid of that twinge of the gout, Tom? Did you rub in that ointment?" while Tom replied: "Ay. How about that rheumatism of yours? Have you tried that Indy oil?" receiving a like assurance.

The remainder of the Port ebbed in meditation and chance remarks. The bit of storm had done them both good; and Tom especially—the cynical, carping, grim old gentleman—was much improved by the nearer resemblance of his manner to Andrew's.

Behind this unaffected fraternal concord, however, the fact that they were pledged to a race in eccentricity, was present. They had been rivals before; and anterior to the date of his marriage, Andrew had done odd eclipsing things. But Andrew required prompting to it; he required to be put upon his mettle. Whereas, it was more nature with Tom: nature and the absence of a wife, gave him advantages over Andrew. Besides, he had his character to maintain. He had said the word: and the first vanity of your born eccentric is, that he shall be taken for infallible.

Presently Andrew ducked his head to mark the evening clouds flushing over the court-yard of the Aurora.

"Time to be off, Tom," he said: "wife at home."

"Ah!" Tom answered. "Well, I haven't got to go to bed so early."

"What an old rogue you are, Tom!" Andrew pushed his elbows forward on the table amiably. "'Gad, we haven't drunk wine together since—by George! we'll have another pint."

"Many as you like," said Tom.

Over the succeeding pint, Andrew, in whose veins the Port was merry, favoured his brother with an imitation of Major Strike, and indicated his dislike to that officer. Tom informed him that Major Strike was speculating.

"The ass eats at my table, and treats me with contempt."

"Just tell him that you're putting by the bones for him. He'll want 'em."

Then Andrew with another glance at the clouds, now violet on a grey sky, said he must really be off. Upon which Tom observed: "Don't come here again."

"You old rascal, Tom!" cried Andrew, swinging over the table: "it's quite jolly for us to be hob-a-nobbing together once more. 'Gad!—no, we won't though! I promised—Harriet. Eh? What say, Tom?"

"Nother pint, Nan?"

Tom shook his head in a roguishly-cosy, irresistible way. Andrew, from a shake of denial and resolve, fell into the same; and there sat the two brothers—a jolly picture.

The hour was ten, when Andrew Cogglesby, comforted by Tom's remark, that he, Tom, had a wig, and that he, Andrew, would have a wigging, left the Aurora; and he left it singing a song. Tom Cogglesby still sat at his table, holding before him Evan's letter, of which he had got possession; and knocking it round and round with a stroke of the forefinger, to the tune of, "Tinker, tailor, soldier, sailor, 'pothecary, ploughboy, thief"; each profession being sounded as a corner presented itself to the point of his nail. After indulging in this species of incantation for some length of time, Tom Cogglesby read the letter from beginning to end, and called peremptorily for pen, ink, and paper.

CHAPTER IX
THE COUNTESS IN LOW SOCIETY

By dint of stratagems worthy of a Court intrigue, the Countess de Saldar contrived to traverse the streets of Lymport, and enter the house where she was born, unsuspected and unseen, under cover of a profusion of lace and veil and mantilla, which only her heroic resolve to keep her beauties hidden from the profane townspeople could have rendered endurable beneath the fervid summer sun. Dress in a foreign style she must, as without it she lost that sense of superiority, which was the only comfort to her in her tribulations. The period of her arrival was ten days subsequent to the burial of her father. She had come in the coach, like any common mortal, and the coachman, upon her request, had put her down at the Governor's house, and the guard had knocked at the door, and the servant had informed her that General Hucklebridge was not the governor of Lymport, nor did Admiral Combleman then reside in the town; which tidings, the coach then being out of sight, it did not disconcert the Countess to hear; and she reached her mother, having, at least, cut off communication with the object of conveyance.

The Countess kissed her mother, kissed Mrs. Fiske, and asked sharply for Evan. Mrs. Fiske let her know that Evan was in the house.

"Where?" inquired the Countess. "I have news of the utmost importance for him. I must see him."

"Where is he, aunt?" said Mrs. Fiske. "In the shop, I think; I wonder he did not see you passing, Louisa."

The Countess went bolt down into a chair.

"Go to him, Jane," said Mrs. Mel. "Tell him Louisa is here, and don't return."

Mrs. Fiske departed, and the Countess smiled.

"Thank you, Mama! you know I never could bear that odious, vulgar little woman. Oh, the heat! You talk of Portugal! And, oh! poor dear Papa! what I have suffered!"

Flapping her laces for air, and wiping her eyes for sorrow, the Countess poured a flood of sympathy into her mother's ears and then said:

"But you have made a great mistake, Mama, in allowing Evan to put his foot into that place. He—beloved of an heiress! Why, if an enemy should hear of it, it would ruin him—positively blast him—for ever. And that she loves him I have proof positive. Yes; with all her frankness, the little thing cannot conceal that from me now. She loves him! And I desire you to guess, Mama, whether rivals will not abound? And what enemy so much to be dreaded as a rival? And what revelation so awful as that he has stood in a—in a—boutique?"

Mrs. Mel maintained her usual attitude for listening. It had occurred to her that it might do no good to tell the grand lady, her daughter, of Evan's resolution, so she simply said, "It is discipline for him," and left her to speak a private word with the youth.

Timidly the Countess inspected the furniture of the apartment, taking chills at the dingy articles she saw, in the midst of her heat. That she should have sprung from this! The thought was painful; still she could forgive Providence so much. But should it ever be known she had sprung from this! Alas! she felt she never could pardon such a dire betrayal. She had come in good spirits, but the mention of Evan's backsliding had troubled her extremely, and though she did not say to herself, What was the benefit resulting from her father's dying, if Evan would be so base-minded? she thought the thing indefinitely, and was forming the words on her mouth, One Harrington in a shop is equal to all! when Evan appeared alone.

"Why, goodness gracious! where's your moustache?" cried the Countess.

"Gone the way of hair!" said Evan, coldly stooping to her forehead.

"Such a distinction!" the Countess continued, reproachfully. "Why, mon Dieu! one could hardly tell you; as you look now, from the very commonest tradesman—if you were not rather handsome and something of a figure. It's a disguise, Evan—do you know that?"

"And I've parted with it—that's all," said Evan. "No more disguises for me!"

The Countess immediately took his arm, and walked with him to a window. His face was certainly changed. Murmuring that the air of Lymport was bad for him, and that he must leave it instantly, she bade him sit and attend to what she was about to say.

"While you have been here, degenerating, Evan, day by day—as you always do out of my sight—degenerating! no less a word!—I have been slaving in your interests. Yes; I have forced the Jocelyns socially to acknowledge us. I have not slept; I have eaten bare morsels. Do abstinence and vigils clear the wits? I know not! but indeed they have enabled me to do more in a week than would suffice for a lifetime. Hark to me. I have discovered Rose's secret. Si! It is so! Rose loves you. You blush; you blush like a girl. She loves you, and you have let yourself be seen in a shop! Contrast me the two things. Oh! in verity, dreadful as it is, one could almost laugh. But the moment I lose sight of you, my instructions vanish as quickly as that hair on your superior lip, which took such time to perfect. Alas! you must grow it again immediately. Use any perfumer's contrivance. Rowland! I have great faith in Rowland. Without him, I believe, there would have been many bald women committing suicide! You remember the bottle I gave to the Count de Villa Flor? 'Countess,' he said to me, 'you have saved this egg-shell from a crack by helping to cover it'—for so he called his head—the top, you know, was beginning to shine like an egg. And I do fear me he would have done it. Ah! you do not conceive what the dread of baldness is! To a woman death—death is preferable to baldness! Baldness is death! And a wig—a wig! Oh, horror! total extinction is better than to rise again in a wig! But you are young, and play with hair. But I was saying, I went to see the Jocelyns. I was introduced to Sir Franks and his lady and the wealthy grandmother. And I have an invitation for you, Evan—you unmannered boy, that you do not bow! A gentle incline forward of the shoulders, and the eyes fixed softly, your upper lids drooping triflingly, as if you thanked with gentle sincerity, but were indifferent. Well, well, if you will not! An invitation for you to spend part of the autumn at Beckley Court, the ancestral domain, where there will be company the nobles of the land! Consider that. You say it was bold in me to face them after that horrible man committed us on board the vessel? A Harrington is anything but a coward. I did go and because I am devoted to your interests. That very morning, I saw announced in the paper, just beneath poor Andrew's hand, as he held it up at the breakfast-table, reading it, I saw among the deaths, Sir Abraham Harrington, of Torquay, Baronet, of quinsy! Twice that good man has come to my rescue! Oh! I welcomed him as a piece of Providence! I turned and said to Harriet, 'I see they have put poor Papa in the paper.' Harriet was staggered. I took the paper from Andrew, and pointed it to her. She has no readiness. She has had no foreign training. She could not comprehend, and Andrew stood on tiptoe, and peeped. He has a bad cough, and coughed himself black in the face. I attribute it to excessive bad manners and his cold feelings. He left the room. I reproached Harriet. But, oh! the singularity of the excellent fortune of such an event at such a time! It showed that our

Harrington-luck had not forsaken us. I hurried to the Jocelyns instantly. Of course, it cleared away any suspicions aroused in them by that horrible man on board the vessel. And the tears I wept for Sir Abraham, Evan, in verity they were tears of deep and sincere gratitude! What is your mouth knitting the corners at? Are you laughing?"

Evan hastily composed his visage to the melancholy that was no counterfeit in him just then.

"Yes," continued the Countess, easily reassured, "I shall ever feel a debt to Sir Abraham Harrington, of Torquay. I dare say we are related to him. At least he has done us more service than many a rich and titled relative. No one supposes he would acknowledge poor Papa. I can forgive him that, Evan!" The Countess pointed out her finger with mournful and impressive majesty, "As we look down on that monkey, people of rank and consideration in society look on what poor dear Papa was."

This was partly true, for Jacko sat on a chair, in his favourite attitude, copied accurately from the workmen of the establishment at their labour with needle and thread. Growing cognizant of the infamy of his posture, the Countess begged Evan to drive him out of her sight, and took a sniff at her smelling-bottle.

She went on: "Now, dear Van, you would hear of your sweet Rose?"

"Not a word!" Evan hastily answered.

"Why, what does this indicate? Whims! Then you do love?"

"I tell you, Louisa, I don't want to hear a word of any of them," said Evan, with an angry gleam in his eyes. "They are nothing to me, nor I to them. I—my walk in life is not theirs."

"Faint heart! faint heart!" the Countess lifted a proverbial forefinger.

"Thank heaven, I shall have the consolation of not going about, and bowing and smirking like an impostor!" Evan exclaimed.

There was a wider intelligence in the Countess's arrested gaze than she chose to fashion into speech.

"I knew," she said, "I knew how the air of this horrible Lymport would act on you. But while I live, Evan, you shall not sink in the sludge. You, with all the pains I have lavished on you! and with your presence!—for you have a presence, so rare among young men in this England! You, who have been to a Court, and interchanged bows with duchesses, and I know not what besides—nay, I do not accuse you; but if you had not been a mere boy, and an English boy—poor Eugenia herself confessed to me that you had a look—a tender cleaving of the underlids—that made her catch her hand to her heart sometimes: it reminded her so acutely of false Belmaraña. Could you have had a greater compliment than that? You shall not stop here another day!"

"True," said Evan, "for I'm going to London to-night."

"Not to London," the Countess returned, with a conquering glance, "but to Beckley Court—and with me."

"To London, Louisa, with Mr. Goren."

Again the Countess eyed him largely; but took, as it were, a side-path from her broad thought, saying: "Yes, fortunes are made in London, if you would they should be rapid."

She meditated. At that moment Dandy knocked at the door, and called outside: "Please, master, Mr. Goren says there's a gentleman in the shop—wants to see you."

"Very well," replied Evan, moving. He was swung violently round.

The Countess had clutched him by the arm. A fearful expression was on her face.

"Whither do you go?" she said.

"To the shop, Louisa."

Too late to arrest the villanous word, she pulled at him. "Are you quite insane? Consent to be seen by a gentleman there? What has come to you? You must be lunatic! Are we all to be utterly ruined—disgraced?"

"Is my mother to starve?" said Evan.

"Absurd rejoinder! No! You should have sold everything here before this. She can live with Harriet—she—once out of this horrible element—she would not show it. But, Evan, you are getting away from me: you are not going?—speak!"

"I am going," said Evan.

The Countess clung to him, exclaiming: "Never, while I have the power to detain you!" but as he was firm and strong, she had recourse to her woman's aids, and burst into a storm of sobs on his shoulder—a scene of which Mrs. Mel was, for some seconds, a composed spectator.

"What's the matter now?" said Mrs. Mel.

Evan impatiently explained the case. Mrs. Mel desired her daughter to avoid being ridiculous, and making two fools in her family; and at the same time that she told Evan there was no occasion for him to go, contrived, with a look, to make the advice a command. He, in that state of mind when one takes bitter delight in doing an abhorred duty, was hardly willing to be submissive; but the despair of the Countess reduced him, and for her sake he consented to forego the sacrifice of his pride which was now his sad, sole pleasure. Feeling him linger, the Countess relaxed her grasp. Hers were tears that dried as soon as they had served their end; and, to give him the full benefit of his conduct, she said: "I knew Evan would be persuaded by me."

Evan pitifully pressed her hand, and sighed.

"Tea is on the table down-stairs," said Mrs. Mel. "I have cooked something for you, Louisa. Do you sleep here to-night?"

"Can I tell you, Mama?" murmured the Countess. "I am dependent on our Evan."

"Oh! well, we will eat first," said Mrs. Mel, and they went to the table below, the Countess begging her mother to drop titles in designating her to the servants, which caused Mrs. Mel to say:

"There is but one. I do the cooking"; and the Countess, ever disposed to flatter and be suave, even when stung by a fact or a phrase, added:

"And a beautiful cook you used to be, dear Mama!"

At the table, awaiting them, sat Mrs. Wishaw, Mrs. Fiske, and Mr. Goren, who soon found themselves enveloped in the Countess's graciousness. Mr. Goren would talk of trade, and compare Lymport business with London, and the Countess, loftily interested in his remarks, drew him out to disgust her brother. Mrs. Wishaw, in whom the Countess at once discovered a frivolous pretentious woman of the moneyed trading class, she treated as one who was alive to society, and surveyed matters from a station in the world, leading her to think that she tolerated Mr. Goren, as a lady-Christian of the highest rank should tolerate the insects that toil for us. Mrs. Fiske was not so tractable, for Mrs. Fiske was hostile and armed. Mrs. Fiske adored the great Mel, and she had never loved Louisa. Hence, she scorned Louisa on account of her late behaviour toward her dead parent. The Countess saw through her, and laboured to be friendly with her, while she rendered her disagreeable in the eyes of Mrs. Wishaw, and let Mrs. Wishaw perceive that sympathy was possible between them; manoeuvring a trifle too delicate, perhaps, for the people present, but sufficient to blind its keen-witted author to the something that was being concealed from herself, of which something, nevertheless, her senses apprehensively warned her: and they might have spoken to her wits, but that mortals cannot, unaided, guess, or will not, unless struck in the face by the fact, credit, what is to their minds the last horror.

"I came down in the coach, quite accidental, with this gentleman," said Mrs. Wishaw, fanning a cheek and nodding at Mr. Goren. "I'm an old flame of dear Mel's. I knew him when he was an apprentice in London. Now, wasn't it odd? Your mother—I suppose I must call you 'my lady'?"

The Countess breathed a tender "Spare me," with a smile that added, "among friends!"

Mrs. Wishaw resumed: "Your mother was an old flame of this gentleman's, I found out. So there were two old flames, and I couldn't help thinking! But I was so glad to have seen dear Mel once more."

"Ah!" sighed the Countess.

"He was always a martial-looking man, and laid out, he was quite imposing. I declare, I cried so, as it reminded me of when I couldn't have him, for he had nothing but his legs and arms—and I married Wishaw. But it's a comfort to think I have been of some service to dear, dear Mel! for Wishaw's a man of accounts and payments; and I knew Mel had cloth from him, and," the lady suggested bills delayed, with two or three nods, "you know! and I'll do my best for his son."

"You are kind," said the Countess, smiling internally at the vulgar creature's misconception of Evan's requirements.

"Did he ever talk much about Mary Fence?" asked Mrs. Wishaw. "'Polly Fence,' he used to say, 'sweet Polly Fence!'"

"Oh! I think so. Frequently," observed the Countess.

Mrs. Fiske primmed her mouth. She had never heard the great Mel allude to the name of Fence.

The Goren-croak was heard:

"Painters have painted out 'Melchisedec' this afternoon. Yes,—ah! In and out—as the saying goes."

Here was an opportunity to mortify the Countess.

Mrs. Fiske placidly remarked: "Have we the other put up in its stead? It's shorter."

A twinge of weakness had made Evan request that the name of Evan Harrington should not decorate the shopfront till he had turned his back on it, for a time. Mrs. Mel crushed her venomous niece.

"What have you to do with such things? Shine in your own affairs first, Ann, before you meddle with others."

Relieved at hearing that "Melchisedec" was painted out, and unsuspicious of the announcement that should replace it, the Countess asked Mrs. Wishaw if she thought Evan like her dear Papa.

"So like," returned the lady, "that I would not be alone with him yet, for worlds. I should expect him to be making love to me: for, you know, my dear—I must be familiar—Mel never could be alone with you, without! It was his nature. I speak of him before marriage. But, if I can trust myself with him, I shall take charge of Mr. Evan, and show him some London society."

"That is indeed kind," said the Countess, glad of a thick veil for the utterance of her contempt. "Evan, though—I fear—will be rather engaged. His friends, the Jocelyns of Beckley Court, will—I fear—hardly dispense with him and Lady Splenders—you know her? the Marchioness of Splenders? No?—by repute, at least: a most beautiful and most fascinating woman; report of him alone has induced her to say that Evan must and shall form a part of her autumnal gathering at Splenders Castle. And how he is to get out of it, I cannot tell. But I am sure his multitudinous engagements will not prevent his paying due court to Mistress Wishaw."

As the Countess intended, Mistress Wishaw's vanity was reproved, and her ambition excited: a pretty doublestroke, only possible to dexterous players.

The lady rejoined that she hoped so, she was sure; and forthwith (because she suddenly seemed to possess him more than his son), launched upon Mel's incomparable personal attractions. This caused the Countess to enlarge upon Evan's vast personal prospects. They talked across each other a little, till the Countess remembered her breeding, allowed Mrs. Wishaw to run to an end in hollow exclamations, and put a finish to the undeclared controversy, by a traverse of speech, as if she were taking up the most important subject of their late colloquy. "But Evan is not in his own hands—he is in the hands of a lovely young woman, I must tell you. He belongs to her, and not to us. You have heard of Rose Jocelyn, the celebrated heiress?"

"Engaged?" Mrs. Wishaw whispered aloud.

The Countess, an adept in the lie implied—practised by her, that she might not subject herself to future punishment (in which she was so devout a believer, that she condemned whole hosts to it)—deeply smiled.

"Really!" said Mrs. Wishaw, and was about to inquire why Evan, with these brilliant expectations, could think of trade and tailoring, when the young man, whose forehead had been growing black, jumped up, and quitted them; thus breaking the harmony of the table; and as the Countess had said enough, she turned the conversation to the always welcome theme of low society. She broached death and corpses; and became extremely interesting, and very sympathetic: the only difference between the ghostly anecdotes she related, and those of the other ladies, being that her ghosts were all of them titled, and walked mostly under the burden of a coronet. For instance, there was the Portuguese Marquis de Col. He had married a Spanish wife, whose end was mysterious. Undressing, on the night of the anniversary of her death, and on the point of getting into bed, he beheld the dead woman lying on her back before him. All night long he had to sleep with this freezing phantom! Regularly, every fresh anniversary, he had to endure the same penance, no matter where he might be, or in what strange bed. On one occasion, when he took the live for the dead, a curious thing occurred, which the Countess scrupled less to relate than would men to hint at. Ghosts were the one childish enjoyment Mrs. Mel allowed herself, and she listened to her daughter intently, ready to cap any narrative; but Mrs. Fiske stopped the flood.

"You have improved on Peter Smithers, Louisa," she said.

The Countess turned to her mildly.

"You are certainly thinking of Peter Smithers," Mrs. Fiske continued, bracing her shoulders. "Surely, you remember poor Peter, Louisa? An old flame of your own! He was going to kill himself, but married a Devonshire woman, and they had disagreeables, and SHE died, and he was undressing, and saw her there in the bed, and wouldn't get into it, and had the mattress, and the curtains, and the counterpanes, and everything burnt. He told us it himself. You must remember it, Louisa?"

The Countess remembered nothing of the sort. No doubt could exist of its having been the Portuguese Marquis de Col, because he had confided to her the whole affair, and indeed come to her, as his habit was, to ask her what he could possibly do, under the circumstances. If Mrs. Fiske's friend, who married the Devonshire person, had seen the same thing, the coincidence was yet more extraordinary than the case. Mrs. Fiske said it assuredly was, and glanced at her aunt, who, as the Countess now rose, declaring she must speak to Evan, chid Mrs. Fiske, and wished her and Peter Smithers at the bottom of the sea.

"No, no, Mama," said the Countess, laughing, "that would hardly be proper," and before Mrs. Fiske could reply, escaped to complain to Evan of the vulgarity of those women.

She was not prepared for the burst of wrath with which Evan met her. "Louisa," said he, taking her wrist sternly, "you have done a thing I can't forgive. I find it hard to bear disgrace myself: I will not consent to bring it upon others. Why did you dare to couple Miss Jocelyn's name with mine?"

The Countess gave him out her arm's length. "Speak on, Van," she said, admiring him with a bright gaze.

"Answer me, Louisa; and don't take me for a fool any more," he pursued. "You have coupled Miss Jocelyn's name with mine, in company, and I insist now upon your giving me your promise to abstain from doing it anywhere, before anybody."

"If she saw you at this instant, Van," returned the incorrigible Countess, "would she desire it, think you? Oh! I must make you angry before her, I see that! You have your father's frown. You surpass him, for your delivery is more correct, and equally fluent. And if a woman is momentarily melted by softness in a man, she is for ever subdued by boldness and bravery of mien."

Evan dropped her hand. "Miss Jocelyn has done me the honour to call me her friend. That was in other days." His lip quivered. "I shall not see Miss Jocelyn again. Yes; I would lay down my life for her; but that's idle talk. No such chance will ever come to me. But I can save her from being spoken of in alliance with me, and what I am, and I tell you, Louisa, I will not have it." Saying which, and while he looked harshly at her, wounded pride bled through his eyes.

She was touched. "Sit down, dear; I must explain to you, and make you happy against your will," she said, in another voice, and an English accent. "The mischief is done, Van. If you do not want Rose Jocelyn to love you, you must undo it in your own way. I am not easily deceived. On the morning I went to her house in town, she took me aside, and spoke to me. Not a confession in words. The blood in her cheeks, when I mentioned you, did that for her. Everything about you she must know—how you bore your grief, and all. And not in her usual free manner, but timidly, as if she feared a surprise, or feared to be wakened to the secret in her bosom she half suspects—'Tell him!' she said, 'I hope he will not forget me.'"

The Countess was interrupted by a great sob; for the picture of frank Rose Jocelyn changed, and soft, and, as it were, shadowed under a veil of bashful regard for him, so filled the young man with sorrowful tenderness, that he trembled, and was as a child.

Marking the impression she had produced on him, and having worn off that which he had produced on her, the Countess resumed the art in her style of speech, easier to her than nature.

"So the sweetest of Roses may be yours, dear Van; and you have her in a gold setting, to wear on your heart. Are you not enviable? I will not—no, I will not tell you she is perfect. I must fashion the sweet young creature.

Though I am very ready to admit that she is much improved by this—shall I call it, desired consummation?"

Evan could listen no more. Such a struggle was rising in his breast: the effort to quench what the Countess had so shrewdly kindled; passionate desire to look on Rose but for one lightning flash: desire to look on her, and muffled sense of shame twin-born with it: wild love and leaden misery mixed: dead hopelessness and vivid hope. Up to the neck in Purgatory, but his soul saturated with visions of Bliss! The fair orb of Love was all that was wanted to complete his planetary state, and aloft it sprang, showing many faint, fair tracts to him, and piling huge darknesses.

As if in search of something, he suddenly went from the room.

"I have intoxicated the poor boy," said the Countess, and consulted an attitude by the evening light in a mirror. Approving the result, she rang for her mother, and sat with her till dark; telling her she could not and would not leave her dear Mama that night. At the supper-table Evan did not appear, and Mr. Goren, after taking counsel of Mrs. Mel, dispersed the news that Evan was off to London. On the road again, with a purse just as ill-furnished, and in his breast the light that sometimes leads gentlemen, as well as ladies, astray.

CHAPTER X
MY GENTLEMAN ON THE ROAD AGAIN

Near a milestone, under the moonlight, crouched the figure of a woman, huddled with her head against her knees, and careless hair falling to the summer's dust. Evan came upon this sight within a few miles of Fallowfield. At first he was rather startled, for he had inherited superstitious emotions from his mother, and the road was lone, the moon full. He went up to her and spoke a gentle word, which provoked no reply. He ventured to put his hand on her shoulder, continuing softly to address her. She was flesh and blood. Evan stooped his head to catch a whisper from her mouth, but nothing save a heavier fall of the breath she took, as of one painfully waking, was heard.

A misery beyond our own is a wholesome picture for youth, and though we may not for the moment compare the deep with the lower deep, we, if we have a heart for outer sorrows, can forget ourselves in it. Evan had just been accusing the heavens of conspiracy to disgrace him. Those patient heavens had listened, as is their wont. They had viewed and had not been disordered by his mental frenzies. It is certainly hard that they do not come down to us, and condescend to tell us what they mean, and be dumb-foundered by the perspicuity of our arguments—the argument, for instance, that they have not fashioned us for the science of the shears, and do yet impel us to wield them. Nevertheless, they to whom mortal life has ceased to be a long matter perceive that our appeals for conviction are answered, now and then very closely upon the call. When we have cast off the scales of hope and fancy, and surrender our claims on mad chance, it is given us to see that some plan is working out: that the heavens, icy as they are to the pangs of our blood, have been throughout speaking to our souls; and, according to the strength there existing, we learn to comprehend them. But their language is an element of Time, whom primarily we have to know.

Evan Harrington was young. He wished not to clothe the generation. What was to the remainder of the exiled sons of Adam simply the brand of expulsion from Paradise, was to him hell. In his agony, anything less than an angel, soft-voiced in his path, would not have satisfied the poor boy, and here was this wretched outcast, and instead of being relieved, he was to act the reliever!

Striving to rouse the desolate creature, he shook her slightly. She now raised her head with a slow, gradual motion, like that of a wax-work, showing a white young face, tearless,—dreadfully drawn at the lips. After gazing at him, she turned her head mechanically to her shoulder, as to ask him why he touched her. He withdrew his hand, saying:

"Why are you here? Pardon me; I want, if possible, to help you."

A light sprang in her eyes. She jumped from the stone, and ran forward a step or two, with a gasp:

"Oh, my God! I want to go and drown myself."

Evan lingered behind her till he saw her body sway, and in a fit of trembling she half fell on his outstretched arm. He led her to the stone, not knowing what on earth to do with her. There was no sign of a house near; they were quite solitary; to all his questions she gave an unintelligible moan. He had not the heart to leave her, so, taking a sharp seat on a heap of flints, thus possibly furnishing future occupation for one of his craftsmen, he waited, and amused himself by marking out diagrams with his stick in the thick dust.

His thoughts were far away, when he heard, faintly uttered:

"Why do you stop here?"

"To help you."

"Please don't. Let me be. I can't be helped."

"My good creature," said Evan, "it's quite impossible that I should leave you in this state. Tell me where you were going when your illness seized you?"

"I was going," she commenced vacantly, "to the sea—the water," she added, with a shivering lip.

The foolish youth asked her if she could be cold on such a night.

"No, I'm not cold," she replied, drawing closer over her lap the ends of a shawl which would in that period have been thought rather gaudy for her station.

"You were going to Lymport?"

"Yes,—Lymport's nearest, I think."

"And why were you out travelling at this hour?"

She dropped her head, and began rocking to right and left.

While they talked the noise of waggon-wheels was heard approaching. Evan went into the middle of the road, and beheld a covered waggon, and a fellow whom he advanced to meet, plodding a little to the rear of the horses. He proved kindly. He was a farmer's man, he said, and was at that moment employed in removing the furniture of the farmer's son, who had failed as a corn-chandler in Lymport, to Hillford, which he expected to reach about morn. He answered Evan's request that he would afford the young woman conveyance as far as Fallowfield:

"Tak' her in? That I will.

"She won't hurt the harses," he pursued, pointing his whip at the vehicle: "there's my mate, Garge Stoakes, he's in there, snorin' his turn. Can't you hear 'n asnorin' thraugh the wheels? I can; I've been laughin'! He do snore that loud—Garge do!"

Proceeding to inform Evan how George Stokes had snored in that characteristic manner from boyhood, ever since he and George had slept in a hayloft together; and how he, kept wakeful and driven to distraction by George Stokes' nose, had been occasionally compelled, in sheer self-defence, madly to start up and hold that pertinacious alarum in tight compression between thumb and forefinger; and how George Stokes, thus severely handled, had burst his hold with a tremendous snort, as big as a bull, and had invariably uttered the exclamation, "Hulloa!—same to you, my lad!" and rolled over to snore as fresh as ever;—all this with singular rustic comparisons, racy of the soil, and in raw Hampshire dialect, the waggoner came to a halt opposite the stone, and, while Evan strode to assist the girl, addressed himself to the great task of arousing the sturdy sleeper and quieting his trumpet, heard by all ears now that the accompaniment of the wheels was at an end.

George, violently awakened, complained that it was before his time, to which he was true; and was for going off again with exalted contentment, though his heels had been tugged, and were dangling some length out of the machine; but his comrade, with a determined blow of the lungs, gave another valiant pull, and George Stokes was on his legs, marvelling at the world and man. Evan had less difficulty with the girl. She rose to meet him, put up her arms for him to clasp her waist, whispering sharply in an inward breath: "What are you going to do with me?" and indifferent to his verbal response, trustingly yielded her limbs to his guidance. He could see blood on her bitten underlip; as, with the help of the waggoner, he lifted her on the mattress, backed by a portly bundle, which the sagacity of Mr. Stokes had selected for his couch.

The waggoner cracked his whip, laughing at George Stokes, who yawned and settled into a composed ploughswing, without asking questions; apparently resolved to finish his nap on his legs.

"Warn't he like that Myzepper chap, I see at the circus, bound athert gray mare!" chuckled the waggoner. "So he'd 'a gone on, had ye 'a let 'n. No wulves waddn't wake Garge till he'd slept it out. Then he'd say, 'marnin'!' to 'm. Are ye 'wake now, Garge?"

The admirable sleeper preferred to be a quiet butt, and the waggoner leisurely exhausted the fun that was to be had out of him; returning to it with a persistency that evinced more concentration than variety in his mind. At last Evan said: "Your pace is rather slow. They'll be shut up in Fallowfield. I'll go on ahead. You'll find me at one of the inns—the Green Dragon."

In return for this speech, the waggoner favoured him with a stare, followed by the exclamation:

"Oh, no! dang that!"

"Why, what's the matter?" quoth Evan.

"You en't goin' to be off, for to leave me and Garge in the lurch there, with that ther' young woman, in that ther' pickle!" returned the waggoner.

Evan made an appeal to his reason, but finding that impregnable, he pulled out his scanty purse to guarantee his sincerity with an offer of pledgemoney. The waggoner waved it aside. He wanted no money, he said.

"Look heer," he went on; "if you're for a start, I tells ye plain, I chucks that ther' young woman int' the road."

Evan bade him not to be a brute.

"Nark and crop!" the waggoner doggedly ejaculated.

Very much surprised that a fellow who appeared sound at heart, should threaten to behave so basely, Evan asked an explanation: upon which the waggoner demanded to know what he had eyes for: and as this query failed to enlighten the youth, he let him understand that he was a man of family experience, and that it was easy to tell at a glance that the complaint the young woman laboured under was one common to the daughters of Eve. He added that, should an emergency arise, he, though a family man, would be useless: that he always vacated the premises while those incidental scenes were being enacted at home; and that for him and George Stokes to be left alone with the young woman, why they would be of no more service to her than a couple of babies newborn themselves. He, for his part, he assured Evan, should take to his heels, and relinquish waggon, and horses, and all; while George probably would stand and gape; and the end of it would be, they would all be had up for murder. He diverged from the alarming prospect, by a renewal of the foregoing alternative to the gentleman who had constituted himself the young woman's protector. If he parted company with them, they would immediately part company with the young woman, whose condition was evident.

"Why, couldn't you tall that?" said the waggoner, as Evan, tingling at the ears, remained silent.

"I know nothing of such things," he answered, hastily, like one hurt.

I have to repeat the statement, that he was a youth, and a modest one. He felt unaccountably, unreasonably, but horridly, ashamed. The thought of his actual position swamped the sickening disgust at tailordom. Worse, then, might happen to us in this extraordinary world! There was something more abhorrent than sitting with one's legs crossed, publicly stitching, and scoffed at! He called vehemently to the waggoner to whip the horses, and hurry ahead into Fallowfield; but that worthy, whatever might be his dire alarms, had a regular pace, that was conscious of no spur: the reply of "All right!" satisfied him at least; and Evan's chaste sighs for the appearance of an assistant petticoat round a turn of the road, were offered up duly, to the measure of the waggoner's steps.

Suddenly the waggoner came to a halt, and said "Blest if that Garge bain't a snorin' on his pins!"

Evan lingered by him with some curiosity, while the waggoner thumped his thigh to, "Yes he be! no he bain't!" several times, in eager hesitation.

"It's a fellow calling from the downs," said Evan.

"Ay, so!" responded the waggoner. "Dang'd if I didn't think 'twere that Garge of our'n. Hark awhile."

At a repetition of the call, the waggoner stopped his team. After a few minutes, a man appeared panting on the bank above them, down which he ran precipitately, knocked against Evan, apologized with the little breath that remained to him, and then held his hand as to entreat a hearing. Evan thought him half-mad; the waggoner was about to imagine him the victim of a midnight assault. He undeceived them by requesting, in rather flowery terms, conveyance on the road and rest for his limbs. It being explained to him that the waggon was already occupied, he comforted himself aloud with the reflection that it was something to be on the road again for one who had been belated, lost, and wandering over the downs for the last six hours.

"Walcome to git in, when young woman gits out," said the waggoner. "I'll gi' ye my sleep on t' Hillford."

"Thanks, worthy friend," returned the new comer. "The state of the case is this—I'm happy to take from humankind whatsoever I can get. If this gentleman will accept of my company, and my legs hold out, all will yet be well."

Though he did not wear a petticoat, Evan was not sorry to have him. Next to the interposition of the Gods, we pray for human fellowship when we are in a mess. So he mumbled politely, dropped with him a little to the rear, and they all stepped out to the crack of the waggoner's whip.

"Rather a slow pace," said Evan, feeling bound to converse.

"Six hours on the downs makes it extremely suitable to me," rejoined the stranger.

"You lost your way?"

"I did, sir. Yes; one does not court those desolate regions wittingly. I am for life and society. The embraces of Diana do not agree with my constitution. If classics there be who differ from me, I beg them to take six hours on the downs alone with the moon, and the last prospect of bread and cheese, and a chaste bed, seemingly utterly extinguished. I am cured of my romance. Of course, when I say bread and cheese, I speak figuratively. Food is implied."

Evan stole a glance at his companion.

"Besides," the other continued, with an inflexion of grandeur, "for a man accustomed to his hunters, it is, you will confess, unpleasant—I speak hypothetically—to be reduced to his legs to that extent that it strikes him shrewdly he will run them into stumps."

The stranger laughed.

The fair lady of the night illumined his face, like one who recognized a subject. Evan thought he knew the voice. A curious struggle therein between native facetiousness and an attempt at dignity, appeared to Evan not unfamiliar; and the egregious failure of ambition and triumph of the instinct, helped him to join the stranger in his mirth.

"Jack Raikes?" he said: "surely?"

"The man!" it was answered to him. "But you? and near our old school—Viscount Harrington? These marvels occur, you see—we meet again by night."

Evan, with little gratification at the meeting, fell into their former comradeship; tickled by a recollection of his old schoolfellow's India-rubber mind.

Mr. Raikes stood about a head under him. He had extremely mobile features; thick, flexible eyebrows; a loose, voluble mouth; a ridiculous figure on a dandified foot. He represented to you one who was rehearsing a part he wished to act before the world, and was not aware that he took the world into his confidence.

How he had come there his elastic tongue explained in tropes and puns and lines of dramatic verse. His patrimony spent, he at once believed himself an actor, and he was hissed off the stage of a provincial theatre.

"Ruined, the last ignominy endured, I fled from the gay vistas of the Bench—for they live who would thither lead me! and determined, the day before the yesterday—what think'st thou? why to go boldly, and offer myself as Adlatus to blessed old Cudford! Yes! a little Latin is all that remains to me, and I resolved, like the man I am, to turn, hic, hac, hoc, into bread and cheese, and beer: Impute nought foreign to me, in the matter of pride."

"Usher in our old school—poor old Jack!" exclaimed Evan.

"Lieutenant in the Cudford Academy!" the latter rejoined. "I walked the distance from London. I had my interview with the respected principal. He gave me of mutton nearest the bone, which, they say, is sweetest; and on sweet things you should not regale in excess. Endymion watched the sheep that bred that mutton! He gave me the thin beer of our boyhood, that I might the more soberly state my mission. That beer, my friend, was brewed by one who wished to form a study for pantomimic masks. He listened with the gravity which is all his own to the recital of my career; he pleasantly compared me to Phaethon, congratulated the river Thames at my not setting it on fire in my rapid descent, and extended to me the three fingers of affectionate farewell. 'You an usher, a rearer of youth, Mr. Raikes? Oh, no! Oh, no!' That was all I could get out of him. 'Gad! he might have seen that I didn't joke with the mutton-bone. If I winced at the beer it was imperceptible. Now a man who can do that is what I call a man in earnest."

"You've just come from Cudford?" said Evan.

"Short is the tale, though long the way, friend Harrington. From Bodley is ten miles to Beckley. I walked them. From Beckley is fifteen miles to Fallowfield. Them I was traversing, when, lo! near sweet eventide a fair horsewoman riding with her groom at her horse's heels. 'Lady,' says I, addressing her, as much out of the style of the needy as possible, 'will you condescend to direct me to Fallowfield?'—'Are you going to the match?' says she. I answered boldly that I was. 'Beckley's in,' says she, 'and you'll be in time to see them out, if you cut across the downs there.' I lifted my hat—a desperate measure, for the brim won't bear much—but honour to women though we perish. She bowed: I cut across the downs. In fine, Harrington, old boy, I've been wandering among those downs for the last seven or eight hours. I was on the point of turning my back on the road for the twentieth time, I believe when I heard your welcome vehicular music, and hailed you; and I ask you, isn't it luck for a fellow who hasn't got a penny in his pocket, and is as hungry as five hundred hunters, to drop on an old friend like this?"

Evan answered with the question:

"Where was it you said you met the young lady?"

"In the first place, O Amadis! I never said she was young. You're on the scent, I see."

Nursing the fresh image of his darling in his heart's recesses, Evan, as they entered Fallowfield, laid the state of his purse before Jack, and earned anew the epithet of Amadis, when it came to be told that the occupant of the waggon was likewise one of its pensioners.

Sleep had long held its reign in Fallowfield. Nevertheless, Mr. Raikes, though blind windows alone looked on him, and nought foreign was to be imputed to him in the matter of pride, had become exceedingly solicitous concerning his presentation to the inhabitants of that quiet little country town; and while Evan and the waggoner consulted—the former with regard to the chances of procuring beds and supper, the latter as to his prospect of beer and a comfortable riddance of the feminine burden weighing on them all—Mr. Raikes was engaged in persuading his hat to assume something of the gentlemanly polish of its youth, and might have been observed now and then furtively catching up a leg to be dusted. Ere the wheels of the waggon stopped he had gained that ease of mind which the knowledge that you have done all a man may do and circumstances warrant, establishes. Capacities conscious of their limits may repose even proudly when they reach them; and, if Mr. Raikes had not quite the air of one come out of a bandbox, he at least proved to the discerning intelligence that he knew what sort of manner befitted that happy occasion, and was enabled by the pains he had taken to glance with a challenge at the sign of the hostelry, under which they were now ranked, and from which, though the hour was late, and Fallowfield a singularly somnolent little town, there issued signs of life approaching to festivity.

CHAPTER XI
DOINGS AT AN INN

What every traveller sighs to find, was palatably furnished by the Green Dragon of Fallowfield—a famous inn, and a constellation for wandering coachmen. There pleasant smiles seasoned plenty, and the bill was gilded in a manner unknown to our days. Whoso drank of the ale of the Green Dragon kept in his memory a place apart for it. The secret, that to give a warm welcome is the breath of life to an inn, was one the Green Dragon boasted, even then, not to share with many Red Lions, or Cocks of the Morning, or Kings' Heads, or other fabulous monsters; and as if to show that when you are in the right track you are sure to be seconded, there was a friend of the Green Dragon, who, on a particular night of the year, caused its renown to enlarge to the dimensions of a miracle. But that, for the moment, is my secret.

Evan and Jack were met in the passage by a chambermaid. Before either of them could speak, she had turned and fled, with the words:

"More coming!" which, with the addition of "My goodness me!" were echoed by the hostess in her recess. Hurried directions seemed to be consequent, and then the hostess sallied out, and said, with a curtsey:

"Please to step in, gentlemen. This is the room, tonight."

Evan lifted his hat; and bowing, requested to know whether they could have a supper and beds.

"Beds, Sir!" cried the hostess. "What am I to do for beds! Yes, beds indeed you may have, but bed-rooms—if you ask for them, it really is more than I can supply you with. I have given up my own. I sleep with my maid Jane to-night."

"Anything will do for us, madam," replied Evan, renewing his foreign courtesy. "But there is a poor young woman outside."

"Another!" The hostess instantly smiled down her inhospitable outcry.

"She," said Evan, "must have a room to herself. She is ill."

"Must is must, sir," returned the gracious hostess. "But I really haven't the means."

"You have bed-rooms, madam?"

"Every one of them engaged, sir."

"By ladies, madam?"

"Lord forbid, Sir!" she exclaimed with the honest energy of a woman who knew her sex.

Evan bade Jack go and assist the waggoner to bring in the girl. Jack, who had been all the time pulling at his wristbands, and settling his coat-collar by the dim reflection of a window of the bar, departed, after, on his own authority, assuring the hostess that fever was not the young woman's malady, as she protested against admitting fever into her house, seeing that she had to consider her guests.

"We're open to all the world to-night, except fever," said the hostess. "Yes," she rejoined to Evan's order that the waggoner and his mate should be supplied with ale, "they shall have as much as they can drink," which is not a speech usual at inns, when one man gives an order for others, but Evan passed it by, and politely begged to be shown in to one of the gentlemen who had engaged bedrooms.

"Oh! if you can persuade any of them, sir, I'm sure I've nothing to say," observed the hostess. "Pray, don't ask me to stand by and back it, that's all."

Had Evan been familiar with the Green Dragon, he would have noticed that the landlady, its presiding genius, was stiffer than usual; the rosy smile was more constrained, as if a great host had to be embraced, and were trying it to the utmost stretch. There was, however, no asperity about her, and when she had led him to the door he was to enter to prefer his suit, and she had asked whether the young woman was quite common, and he had replied that he had picked her up on the road, and that she was certainly poor, the hostess said:

"I'm sure you're a very good gentleman, sir, and if I could spare your asking at all, I would."

With that she went back to encounter Mr. Raikes and his charge, and prime the waggoner and his mate.

A noise of laughter and talk was stilled gradually, as Evan made his bow into a spacious room, wherein, as the tops of pines are seen swimming on the morning mist, about a couple of dozen guests of divers conditions sat partially revealed through wavy clouds of tobacco-smoke. By their postures, which Evan's appearance by no means disconcerted, you read in a glance men who had been at ease for so many hours that they had no troubles in the world save the two ultimate perplexities of the British Sybarite, whose bed of roses is harassed by the pair of problems: first, what to do with his legs; secondly, how to imbibe liquor with the slightest possible derangement of those members subordinate to his upper structure. Of old the Sybarite complained. Not so our self-helpful islanders. Since they could not, now that work was done and jollity the game, take off their legs, they got away from them as far as they might, in fashions original or imitative: some by thrusting them out at full length; some by cramping them under their chairs: while some, taking refuge in a mental effort, forgot them, a process to be recommended if it did not involve occasional pangs of consciousness to the legs of their neighbours. We see in our cousins West of the great water, who are said to exaggerate our peculiarities, beings labouring under the same difficulty, and intent on its solution. As to the second problem: that of drinking without discomposure to the subservient limbs: the company present worked out this republican principle ingeniously, but in a manner beneath the attention of the Muse. Let Clio record that mugs and glasses, tobacco and pipes, were strewn upon the table. But if the guests had arrived at that stage when to reach the arm, or arrange the person, for a sip of good stuff, causes moral debates, and presents to the mind impediments equal to what would be raised in active men by the prospect of a great excursion, it is not to be wondered at that the presence of a stranger produced no immediate commotion. Two or three heads were half turned; such as faced him imperceptibly lifted their eyelids.

"Good evening, sir," said one who sat as chairman, with a decisive nod.

"Good night, ain't it?" a jolly-looking old fellow queried of the speaker, in an under-voice.

"'Gad, you don't expect me to be wishing the gentleman good-bye, do you?" retorted the former.

"Ha! ha! No, to be sure," answered the old boy; and the remark was variously uttered, that "Good night," by a caprice of our language, did sound like it.

"Good evening's 'How d' ye do?'—'How are ye?' Good night's 'Be off, and be blowed to you,'" observed an interpreter with a positive mind; and another, whose intelligence was not so clear, but whose perceptions had seized the point, exclaimed: "I never says it when I hails a chap; but, dash my buttons, if I mightn't 'a done, one day or another! Queer!"

The chairman, warmed by his joke, added, with a sharp wink: "Ay; it would be queer, if you hailed 'Good night' in the middle of the day!" and this among a company soaked in ripe ale, could not fail to run the electric circle, and persuaded several to change their positions; in the rumble of which, Evan's reply, if he had made any, was lost. Few, however, were there who could think of him, and ponder on that glimpse of fun, at the same time; and he would have been passed over, had not the chairman said: "Take a seat, sir; make yourself comfortable."

"Before I have that pleasure," replied Evan, "I—"

"I see where 'tis," burst out the old boy who had previously superinduced a diversion: "he's going to ax if he can't have a bed!"

A roar of laughter, and "Don't you remember this day last year?" followed the cunning guess. For awhile explication was impossible; and Evan coloured, and smiled, and waited for them.

"I was going to ask—"

"Said so!" shouted the old boy, gleefully.

"—one of the gentlemen who has engaged a bed-room to do me the extreme favour to step aside with me, and allow me a moment's speech with him."

Long faces were drawn, and odd stares were directed toward him, in reply.

"I see where 'tis"; the old boy thumped his knee. "Ain't it now? Speak up, sir! There's a lady in the case?"

"I may tell you thus much," answered Evan, "that it is an unfortunate young woman, very ill, who needs rest and quiet."

"Didn't I say so?" shouted the old boy. But this time, though his jolly red jowl turned all round to demand a confirmation, it was not generally considered that he had divined so correctly. Between a lady and an unfortunate young woman, there seemed to be a strong distinction, in the minds of the company.

The chairman was the most affected by the communication. His bushy eyebrows frowned at Evan, and he began tugging at the brass buttons of his coat, like one preparing to arm for a conflict.

"Speak out, sir, if you please," he said. "Above board—no asides—no taking advantages. You want me to give up my bed-room for the use of your young woman, sir?"

Evan replied quietly: "She is a stranger to me; and if you could see her, sir, and know her situation, I think she would move your pity."

"I don't doubt it, sir—I don't doubt it," returned the chairman. "They all move our pity. That's how they get over us. She has diddled you, and she would diddle me, and diddle us all—diddle the devil, I dare say, when her time comes. I don't doubt it, sir."

To confront a vehement old gentleman, sitting as president in an assembly of satellites, requires command of countenance, and Evan was not browbeaten: he held him, and the whole room, from where he stood, under a serene and serious eye, for his feelings were too deeply stirred on behalf of the girl to let him think of himself. That question of hers, "What are you going to do with me?" implying such helplessness and trust, was still sharp on his nerves.

"Gentlemen," he said, "I humbly beg your pardon for disturbing you as I do."

But with a sudden idea that a general address on behalf of a particular demand must necessarily fail, he let his eyes rest on one there, whose face was neither stupid nor repellent, and who, though he did not look up, had an attentive, thoughtful cast about the mouth.

"May I entreat a word apart with you, sir?"

Evan was not mistaken in the index he had perused. The gentleman seemed to feel that he was selected from the company, and slightly raising his head, carelessly replied: "My bed is entirely at your disposal," resuming his contemplative pose.

On the point of thanking him, Evan advanced a step, when up started the irascible chairman.

"I don't permit it! I won't allow it!" And before Evan could ask his reasons, he had rung the bell, muttering: "They follow us to our inns, now, the baggages! They must harry us at our inns! We can't have peace and quiet at our inns!—"

In a state of combustion, he cried out to the waiter:

"Here, Mark, this gentleman has brought in a dirty wench: pack her up to my bed-room, and lock her in lock her in, and bring down the key."

Agreeably deceived in the old gentleman's intentions, Evan could not refrain from joining the murmured hilarity created by the conclusion of his order. The latter glared at him, and added: "Now, sir, you've done your worst. Sit down, and be merry."

Replying that he had a friend outside, and would not fail to accept the invitation, Evan retired. He was met by the hostess with the reproachful declaration on her lips, that she was a widow woman, wise in appearances, and that he had brought into her house that night work she did not expect, or bargain for. Rather (since I must speak truth of my gentleman) to silence her on the subject, and save his ears, than to propitiate her favour towards the girl, Evan drew out his constitutionally lean purse, and dropped it in her hand, praying her to put every expense incurred to his charge. She exclaimed:

"If Dr. Pillie has his full sleep this night, I shall be astonished"; and Evan hastily led Jack into the passage to impart to him, that the extent of his resources was reduced to the smallest of sums in shillings.

"I can beat my friend at that reckoning," said Mr. Raikes; and they entered the room.

Eyes were on him. This had ever the effect of causing him to swell to monstrous proportions in the histrionic line. Asking the waiter carelessly for some light supper dish, he suggested the various French, with "not that?" and the affable naming of another. "Nor that? Dear me, we shall have to sup on chops, I believe!"

Evan saw the chairman scrutinizing Raikes, much as he himself might have done, and he said: "Bread and cheese for me."

Raikes exclaimed: "Really? Well, my lord, you lead, and your taste is mine!"

A second waiter scudded past, and stopped before the chairman to say: "If you please, sir, the gentlemen upstairs send their compliments, and will be happy to accept."

"Ha!" was the answer. "Thought better of it, have they! Lay for three more, then. Five more, I guess." He glanced at the pair of intruders.

Among a portion of the guests there had been a return to common talk, and one had observed that he could not get that "Good Evening," and "Good Night," out of his head which had caused a friend to explain the meaning of these terms of salutation to him: while another, of a philosophic turn, pursued the theme: "You see, when we meets, we makes a night of it. So, when we parts, it's Good Night—natural! ain't it?" A proposition assented to, and considerably dilated on; but whether he was laughing at that, or what had aroused the fit, the chairman did not say.

Gentle chuckles had succeeded his laughter by the time the bread and cheese appeared.

In the rear of the provision came three young gentlemen, of whom the foremost lumped in, singing to one behind him, "And you shall have little Rosey!"

They were clad in cricketing costume, and exhibited the health and manners of youthful Englishmen of station. Frolicsome young bulls bursting on an assemblage of sheep, they might be compared to. The chairman welcomed them a trifle snubbingly. The colour mounted to the cheeks of Mr. Raikes as he made incision in the cheese, under their eyes, knitting his brows fearfully, as if at hard work.

The chairman entreated Evan to desist from the cheese; and, pulling out his watch, thundered: "Time!"

The company generally jumped on their legs; and, in the midst of a hum of talk and laughter, he informed Evan and Jack, that he invited them cordially to a supper up-stairs, and would be pleased if they would partake of it, and in a great rage if they would not.

Raikes was for condescending to accept.

Evan sprang up and cried: "Gladly, sir," and gladly would he have cast his cockney schoolmate to the winds, in the presence of these young cricketers; for he had a prognostication.

The door was open, and the company of jolly yeomen, tradesmen, farmers, and the like, had become intent on observing all the ceremonies of precedence: not one would broaden his back on the other; and there was bowing, and scraping, and grimacing, till Farmer Broadmead was hailed aloud, and the old boy stepped forth, and was summarily pushed through: the chairman calling from the rear, "Hulloa! no names to-night!" to which was answered lustily: "All right, Mr. Tom!" and the speaker was reproved with, "There you go! at it again!" and out and up they hustled.

The chairman said quietly to Evan, as they were ascending the stairs: "We don't have names to-night; may as well drop titles." Which presented no peculiar meaning to Evan's mind, and he smiled the usual smile.

To Raikes, at the door of the supper-room, the chairman repeated the same; and with extreme affability and alacrity of abnegation, the other rejoined, "Oh, certainly!"

No wonder that he rubbed his hands with more delight than aristocrats and people with gentlemanly connections are in the habit of betraying at the prospect of refection, for the release from bread and cheese was rendered overpoweringly glorious, in his eyes, by the bountiful contrast exhibited on the board before him.

CHAPTER XII
IN WHICH ALE IS SHOWN TO HAVE ONE QUALITY OF WINE

To proclaim that yon ribs of beef and yonder ruddy Britons have met, is to furnish matter for an hour's comfortable meditation.

Digest the fact. Here the Fates have put their seal to something Nature clearly devised. It was intended; and it has come to pass. A thing has come to pass which we feel to be right! The machinery of the world, then, is not entirely dislocated: there is harmony, on one point, among the mysterious powers who have to do with us.

Apart from its eloquent and consoling philosophy, the picture is pleasant. You see two rows of shoulders resolutely set for action: heads in divers degrees of proximity to their plates: eyes variously twinkling, or hypocritically composed: chaps in vigorous exercise. Now leans a fellow right back with his whole face to the firmament: Ale is his adoration. He sighs not till he sees the end of the mug. Now from one a laugh is sprung; but, as if too early tapped, he turns off the cock, and primes himself anew. Occupied by their own requirements, these Britons allow that their neighbours have rights: no cursing at waste of time is heard when plates have to be passed: disagreeable, it is still duty. Field-Marshal Duty, the Briton's chief star, shines here. If one usurps more than his allowance of elbow-room, bring your charge against them that fashioned him: work away to arrive at some compass yourself.

Now the mustard ceases to travel, and the salt: the guests have leisure to contemplate their achievements. Laughs are more prolonged, and come from the depths.

Now Ale, which is to Beef what Eve was to Adam, threatens to take possession of the field. Happy they who, following Nature's direction, admitted not bright ale into their Paradise till their manhood was strengthened with beef. Some, impatient, had thirsted; had satisfied their thirst; and the ale, the light though lovely spirit, with nothing to hold it down, had mounted to their heads; just as Eve will do when Adam is not mature: just as she did—Alas!

Now, the ruins of the feast being removed, and a clear course left for the flow of ale, Farmer Broadmead, facing the chairman, rises. He stands in an attitude of midway. He speaks:

"Gentlemen! 'Taint fust time you and I be met here, to salbrate this here occasion. I say, not fust time, not by many a time, 'taint. Well, gentlemen, I ain't much of a speaker, gentlemen, as you know. Howsever, here I be. No denyin' that. I'm on my legs. This here's a strange enough world, and a man's a gentleman, I say, we ought for to be glad when we got 'm. You know: I'm coming to it shortly. I ain't much of a speaker, and if you wants somethin' new, you must ax elsewhere: but what I say is—Bang it! here's good health and long life to Mr. Tom, up there!"

"No names!" shouts the chairman, in the midst of a tremendous clatter.

Farmer Broadmead moderately disengages his breadth from the seat. He humbly axes pardon, which is accorded him with a blunt nod.

Ale (to Beef what Eve was to Adam) circulates beneath a dazzling foam, fair as the first woman.

Mr. Tom (for the breach of the rules in mentioning whose name on a night when identities are merged, we offer sincere apologies every other minute), Mr. Tom is toasted. His parents, who selected that day sixty years ago, for his bow to be made to the world, are alluded to with encomiums, and float down to posterity on floods of liquid amber.

But to see all the subtle merits that now begin to bud out from Mr. Tom, the chairman and giver of the feast; and also rightly to appreciate the speeches, we require to be enormously charged with Ale. Mr. Raikes did his best to keep his head above the surface of the rapid flood. He conceived the chairman in brilliant colours, and probably owing to the energy called for by his brain, the legs of the young man failed him twice, as he tried them. Attention was demanded. Mr. Raikes addressed the meeting.

The three young gentlemen-cricketers had hitherto behaved with a certain propriety. It did not offend Mr. Raikes to see them conduct themselves as if they were at a play, and the rest of the company paid actors. He had likewise taken a position, and had been the first to laugh aloud at a particular slip of grammar; while his shrugs at the aspirates transposed and the pronunciation prevalent, had almost established a free-masonry between him and one of the three young gentlemen-cricketers—a fair-haired youth, with a handsome, reckless face, who leaned on the table, humorously eyeing the several speakers, and exchanging by-words and laughs with his friends on each side of him.

But Mr. Raikes had the disadvantage of having come to the table empty in stomach—thirsty exceedingly; and, I repeat, that as, without experience, you are the victim of divinely given Eve, so, with no foundation to receive it upon, are you the victim of good sound Ale. He very soon lost his head. He would otherwise have seen that he must produce a wonderfully-telling speech if he was to keep the position he had taken, and had better not attempt one. The three young cricketers were hostile from the beginning. All of them leant forward, calling attention loudly laughing for the fun to come.

"Gentlemen!" he said: and said it twice. The gap was wide, and he said, "Gentlemen!" again.

This commencement of a speech proves that you have made the plunge, but not that you can swim. At a repetition of "Gentlemen!" expectancy resolved into cynicism.

"Gie'n a help," sang out a son of the plough to a neighbour of the orator.

"Hang it!" murmured another, "we ain't such gentlemen as that comes to."

Mr. Raikes was politely requested to "tune his pipe."

With a gloomy curiosity as to the results of Jack's adventurous undertaking, and a touch of anger at the three whose bearing throughout had displeased him, Evan regarded his friend. He, too, had drunk, and upon emptiness. Bright ale had mounted to his brain. A hero should be held as sacred as the Grand Llama: so let no more be said than that he drank still, nor marked the replenishing of his glass.

Raikes cleared his throat for a final assault: he had got an image, and was dashing off; but, unhappily, as if to make the start seem fair, he was guilty of his reiteration, "Gentlemen."

Everybody knew that it was a real start this time, and indeed he had made an advance, and had run straight through half a sentence. It was therefore manifestly unfair, inimical, contemptuous, overbearing, and base, for one of the three young cricketers at this period to fling back weariedly and exclaim: "By the Lord; too many gentlemen here!"

Evan heard him across the table. Lacking the key of the speaker's previous conduct, the words might have passed. As it was, they, to the ale-invaded head of a young hero, feeling himself the world's equal, and condemned nevertheless to bear through life the insignia of Tailordom, not unnaturally struck with peculiar offence. There was arrogance, too, in the young man who had interposed. He was long in the body, and, when he was not refreshing his sight by a careless contemplation of his finger-nails, looked down on his company at table, as one may do who comes from loftier studies. He had what is popularly known as the nose of our aristocracy: a nose that much culture of the external graces, and affectation of suavity, are required to soften. Thereto were joined thin lips and arched brows. Birth it was possible he could boast, hardly brains. He sat to the right of the fair-haired youth, who, with his remaining comrade, a quiet smiling fellow, appeared to be better liked by the guests, and had been hailed once or twice, under correction of the chairman, as Mr. Harry. The three had distinguished one there by a few friendly passages; and this was he who had offered his bed to Evan for the service of the girl. The recognition they extended to him did not affect him deeply. He was called Drummond, and had his place near the chairmen, whose humours he seemed to relish.

The ears of Mr. Raikes were less keen at the moment than Evan's, but his openness to ridicule was that of a man on his legs solus, amid a company sitting, and his sense of the same—when he saw himself the victim of it—acute. His face was rather comic, and, under the shadow of embarrassment, twitching and working for ideas—might excuse a want of steadiness and absolute gravity in the countenances of others.

The chairman's neighbour, Drummond, whispered him "Laxley will get up a row with that fellow."

"It's young Jocelyn egging him on," said the chairman.

"Um!" added Drummond: "it's the friend of that talkative rascal that's dangerous, if it comes to anything."

Mr. Raikes perceived that his host desired him to conclude. So, lifting his voice and swinging his arm, he ended: "Allow me to propose to you the Fly in Amber. In other words, our excellent host embalmed in brilliant ale! Drink him! and so let him live in our memories for ever!"

He sat down very well contented with himself, very little comprehended, and applauded loudly.

"The Flyin' Number!" echoed Farmer Broadmead, confidently and with clamour; adding to a friend, when both had drunk the toast to the dregs, "But what number that be, or how many 'tis of 'em, dishes me! But that's ne'ther here nor there."

The chairman and host of the evening stood up to reply, welcomed by thunders—"There ye be, Mr. Tom! glad I lives to see ye!" and "No names!" and "Long life to him!"

This having subsided, the chairman spoke, first nodding. "You don't want many words, and if you do, you won't get 'em from me."

Cries of "Got something better!" took up the blunt address.

"You've been true to it, most of you. I like men not to forget a custom."

"Good reason so to be," and "A jolly good custom," replied to both sentences.

"As to the beef, I hope you didn't find it tough: as to the ale—I know all about THAT!"

"Aha! good!" rang the verdict.

"All I can say is, that this day next year it will be on the table, and I hope that every one of you will meet Tom—will meet me here punctually. I'm not a Parliament man, so that'll do."

The chairman's breach of his own rules drowned the termination of his speech in an uproar.

Re-seating himself, he lifted his glass, and proposed: "The Antediluvians!"

Farmer Broadmead echoed: "The Antediloovians!" appending, as a private sentiment, "And dam rum chaps they were!"

The Antediluvians, undoubtedly the toast of the evening, were enthusiastically drunk, and in an ale of treble brew.

When they had quite gone down, Mr. Raikes ventured to ask for the reason of their receiving such honour from a posterity they had so little to do with. He put the question mildly, but was impetuously snapped at by the chairman.

"You respect men for their luck, sir, don't you? Don't be a hypocrite, and say you don't—you do. Very well: so do I. That's why I drink 'The Antediluvians'!"

"Our worthy host here" (Drummond, gravely smiling, undertook to elucidate the case) "has a theory that the constitutions of the Postdiluvians have been deranged, and their lives shortened, by the miasmas of the Deluge. I believe he carries it so far as to say that Noah, in the light of a progenitor, is inferior to Adam, owing to the shaking he had to endure in the ark, and which he conceives to have damaged the patriarch and the nervous systems of his sons. It's a theory, you know."

"They lived close on a thousand years, hale, hearty—and no water!" said the chairman.

"Well!" exclaimed one, some way down the table, a young farmer, red as a cock's comb: "no fools they, eh, master? Where there's ale, would you drink water, my hearty?" and back he leaned to enjoy the tribute to his wit; a wit not remarkable, but nevertheless sufficient in the noise it created to excite the envy of Mr. Raikes, who, inveterately silly when not engaged in a contest, now began to play on the names of the sons of Noah.

The chairman lanced a keen light at him from beneath his bushy eyebrows.

Before long he had again to call two parties to order. To Raikes, Laxley was a puppy: to Laxley, Mr. Raikes was a snob. The antagonism was natural: ale did but put the match to the magazine. But previous to an explosion, Laxley, who had observed Evan's disgust at Jack's exhibition of himself, and had been led to think, by his conduct and clothes in conjunction, that Evan was his own equal; a gentleman condescending to the society of a low-born acquaintance;—had sought with sundry propitiations, intelligent glances, light shrugs, and such like, to divide Evan from Jack. He did this, doubtless, because he partly sympathized with Evan, and to assure him that he took a separate view of him. Probably Evan was already offended, or he held to Jack, as a comrade should, or else it was that Tailordom and the pride of his accepted humiliation bellowed in his ears, every fresh minute: "Nothing assume!" I incline to think that the more ale he drank the fiercer rebel he grew against conventional ideas of rank, and those class-barriers which we scorn so vehemently when we find ourselves kicking at them. Whatsoever the reason that prompted him, he did not respond to Laxley's advances; and Laxley, disregarding him, dealt with Raikes alone.

In a tone plainly directed at him, he said: "Well, Harry, tired of this? The agriculturals are good fun, but I can't stand much of the small cockney. A blackguard who tries to make jokes out of the Scriptures ought to be kicked!"

Harry rejoined, with wet lips: "Wopping stuff, this ale! Who's that you want to kick?"

"Somebody who objects to his bray, I suppose," Mr. Raikes struck in, across the table, negligently thrusting out his elbow to support his head.

"Did you allude to me, sir?" Laxley inquired.

"I alluded to a donkey, sir." Raikes lifted his eyelids to the same level as Laxley's: "a passing remark on that interesting animal."

His friend Harry now came into the ring to try a fall.

"Are you an usher in a school?" he asked, meaning by his looks what men of science in fisticuffs call business.

Mr. Raikes started in amazement. He recovered as quickly.

"No, sir, not quite; but I have no doubt I should be able to instruct you upon a point or two."

"Good manners, for instance?" remarked the third young cricketer, without disturbing his habitual smile.

"Or what comes from not observing them," said Evan, unwilling to have Jack over-matched.

"Perhaps you'll give me a lesson now?" Harry indicated a readiness to rise for either of them.

At this juncture the chairman interposed.

"Harmony, my lads!—harmony to-night."

Farmer Broadmead, imagining it to be the signal for a song, returned:

"All right, Mr.—- Mr. Chair! but we an't got pipes in yet. Pipes before harmony, you know, to-night."

The pipes were summoned forthwith. System appeared to regulate the proceedings of this particular night at the Green Dragon. The pipes charged, and those of the guests who smoked, well fixed behind them, celestial Harmony was invoked through the slowly curling clouds. In Britain the Goddess is coy. She demands pressure to appear, and great gulps of ale. Vastly does she swell the chests of her island children, but with the modesty of a maid at the commencement. Precedence again disturbed the minds of the company. At last the red-faced young farmer led off with "The Rose and the Thorn." In that day Chloe still lived; nor were the amorous transports of Strephon quenched. Mountainous inflation—mouse-like issue characterized the young farmer's first verse. Encouraged by manifest approbation he now told Chloe that he "by Heaven! never would plant in that bosom a thorn," with such a volume of sound as did indeed show how a lover's oath should be uttered in the ear of a British damsel to subdue her.

"Good!" cried Mr. Raikes, anxious to be convivial.

Subsiding into impertinence, he asked Laxley, "Could you tip us a Strephonade, sir? Rejoiced to listen to you, I'm sure! Promise you my applause beforehand."

Harry replied hotly: "Will you step out of the room with me a minute?"

"Have you a confession to make?" quoth Jack, unmoved. "Have you planted a thorn in the feminine flower-garden? Make a clean breast of it at the table. Confess openly and be absolved."

While Evan spoke a word of angry reproof to Raikes, Harry had to be restrained by his two friends. The rest of the company looked on with curiosity; the mouth of the chairman was bunched. Drummond had his eyes on Evan, who was gazing steadily at the three. Suddenly "The fellow isn't a gentleman!" struck the attention of Mr. Raikes with alarming force.

Raikes—and it may be because he knew he could do more than Evan in this respect—vociferated: "I'm the son of a gentleman!"

Drummond, from the head of the table, saw that a diversion was imperative. He leaned forward, and with a look of great interest said:

"Are you? Pray, never disgrace your origin, then."

"If the choice were offered me, I think I would rather have known his father," said the smiling fellow, yawning, and rocking on his chair.

"You would, possibly, have been exceedingly intimate—with his right foot," said Raikes.

The other merely remarked: "Oh! that is the language of the son of a gentleman."

The tumult of irony, abuse, and retort, went on despite the efforts of Drummond and the chairman. It was odd; for at Farmer Broadmead's end of the table, friendship had grown maudlin: two were seen in a drowsy embrace, with crossed pipes; and others were vowing deep amity, and offering to fight the man that might desire it.

"Are ye a friend? or are ye a foe?" was heard repeatedly, and consequences to the career of the respondent, on his choice of affirmatives to either of these two interrogations, emphatically detailed.

It was likewise asked, in reference to the row at the gentlemen's end: "Why doan' they stand up and have 't out?"

"They talks, they speechifies—why doan' they fight for 't, and then be friendly?"

"Where's the yarmony, Mr. Chair, I axes—so please ye?" sang out Farmer Broadmead.

"Ay, ay! Silence!" the chairman called.

Mr. Raikes begged permission to pronounce his excuses, but lapsed into a lamentation for the squandering of property bequeathed to him by his respected uncle, and for which—as far as he was intelligible—he persisted in calling the three offensive young cricketers opposite to account.

Before he could desist, Harmony, no longer coy, burst on the assembly from three different sources. "A Man who is given to Liquor," soared aloft with "The Maid of sweet Seventeen," who participated in the adventures of "Young Molly and the Kicking Cow"; while the guests selected the chorus of the song that first demanded it.

Evan probably thought that Harmony was herself only when she came single, or he was wearied of his fellows, and wished to gaze a moment on the skies whose arms were over and around his young beloved. He went to the window and threw it up, and feasted his sight on the moon standing on the downs. He could have wept at the bitter ignominy that severed him from Rose. And again he gathered his pride as a cloak, and defied the world, and gloried in the sacrifice that degraded him. The beauty of the night touched him, and mixed these feelings with mournfulness. He quite forgot the bellow and clatter behind. The beauty of the night, and heaven knows what treacherous hope in the depths of his soul, coloured existence warmly.

He was roused from his reverie by an altercation unmistakeably fierce.

Raikes had been touched on a tender point. In reply to a bantering remark of his, Laxley had hummed over bits of his oration, amid the chuckles of his comrades. Unfortunately at a loss for a biting retort, Raikes was reduced to that plain confession of a lack of wit; he offered combat.

"I'll tell you what," said Laxley, "I never soil my hands with a blackguard; and a fellow who tries to make fun of Scripture, in my opinion is one. A blackguard—do you hear? But, if you'll give me satisfactory proofs that you really are what I have some difficulty in believing—the son of a gentleman—I'll meet you when and where you please."

"Fight him, anyhow," said Harry. "I'll take him myself after we finish the match to-morrow."

Laxley rejoined that Mr. Raikes must be left to him.

"Then I'll take the other," said Harry. "Where is he?"

Evan walked round to his place.

"I am here," he answered, "and at your service."

"Will you fight?" cried Harry.

There was a disdainful smile on Evan's mouth, as he replied: "I must first enlighten you. I have no pretensions to your blue blood, or yellow. If, sir, you will deign to challenge a man who is not the son of a gentleman, and consider the expression of his thorough contempt for your conduct sufficient to enable you to overlook that fact, you may dispose of me. My friend here has, it seems, reason to be proud of his connections. That you may not subsequently bring the charge against me of having led you to 'soil your hands'—as your friend there terms it—I, with all the willingness in the world to chastise you or him for your impertinence, must first give you a fair chance of escape, by telling you that my father was a tailor."

The countenance of Mr. Raikes at the conclusion of this speech was a painful picture. He knocked the table passionately, exclaiming:

"Who'd have thought it?"

Yet he had known it. But he could not have thought it possible for a man to own it publicly.

Indeed, Evan could not have mentioned it, but for hot fury and the ale. It was the ale in him expelling truth; and certainly, to look at him, none would have thought it.

"That will do," said Laxley, lacking the magnanimity to despise the advantage given him, "you have chosen the very best means of saving your skins."

"We'll come to you when our supply of clothes runs short," added Harry. "A snip!"

"Pardon me!" said Evan, with his eyes slightly widening, "but if you come to me, I shall no longer give you a choice of behaviour. I wish you good-night, gentlemen. I shall be in this house, and am to be found here, till ten o'clock to-morrow morning. Sir," he addressed the chairman, "I must apologize to you for this interruption to your kindness, for which I thank you very sincerely. It's 'good-night,' now, sir," he pursued, bowing, and holding out his hand, with a smile.

The chairman grasped it: "You're a hot-headed young fool, sir: you're an ill-tempered ferocious young ass. Can't you see another young donkey without joining company in kicks-eh? Sit down, and don't dare to spoil the fun any more. You a tailor! Who'll believe it? You're a nobleman in disguise. Didn't your friend say so?—ha! ha! Sit down." He pulled out his watch, and proclaiming that he was born into this world at the hour about to strike, called for a bumper all round.

While such of the company as had yet legs and eyes unvanquished by the potency of the ale, stood up to drink and cheer, Mark, the waiter, scurried into the room, and, to the immense stupefaction of the chairman, and amusement of his guests, spread the news of the immediate birth of a little stranger on the premises, who was declared by Dr. Pillie to be a lusty boy, and for whom the kindly landlady solicited good luck to be drunk.

CHAPTER XIII
THE MATCH OF FALLOW FIELD AGAINST BECKLEY

The dramatic proportions to which ale will exalt the sentiments within us, and our delivery of them, are apt to dwindle and shrink even below the natural elevation when we look back on them from the hither shore of the river of sleep—in other words, wake in the morning: and it was with no very self-satisfied emotions that Evan, dressing by the full light of day, reviewed his share in the events of the preceding night. Why, since he had accepted his fate, should he pretend to judge the conduct of people his superiors in rank? And where was the necessity for him to thrust the fact of his being that abhorred social pariah down the throats of an assembly of worthy good fellows? The answer was, that he had not accepted his fate: that he considered himself as good a gentleman as any man living, and was in absolute hostility with the prejudices of society. That was the state of the case: but the evaporation of ale in his brain caused him to view his actions from the humble extreme of that delightful liquor, of which the spirit had flown and the corpse remained.

Having revived his system with soda-water, and finding no sign of his antagonist below, Mr. Raikes, to disperse the sceptical dimples on his friend's face, alluded during breakfast to a determination he had formed to go forth and show on the cricket-field.

"For, you know," he observed, "they can't have any objection to fight one."

Evan, slightly colouring, answered: "Why, you said up-stairs, you thought fighting duels disgraceful folly."

"So it is, so it is; everybody knows that," returned Jack; "but what can a gentleman do?"

"Be a disgraceful fool, I suppose," said Evan: and Raikes went on with his breakfast, as if to be such occasionally was the distinguished fate of a gentleman, of which others, not so happy in their birth, might well be envious.

He could not help betraying that he bore in mind the main incidents of the festival over-night; for when he had inquired who it might be that had reduced his friend to wear mourning, and heard that it was his father (spoken by Evan with a quiet sigh), Mr. Raikes tapped an egg, and his flexible brows exhibited a whole Bar of contending arguments within. More than for the love of pleasure, he had spent his money to be taken for a gentleman. He naturally thought highly of the position, having bought it. But Raikes appreciated a capital fellow, and felt warmly to Evan, who, moreover, was feeding him.

If not born a gentleman, this Harrington had the look of one, and was pleasing in female eyes, as the landlady, now present, bore witness, wishing them good morning, and hoping they had slept well. She handed to Evan his purse, telling him she had taken it last night, thinking it safer for the time being in her pocket; and that the chairman of the feast paid for all in the Green Dragon up to twelve that day, he having been born between the hours, and liking to make certain: and that every year he did the same; and was a seemingly rough old gentleman, but as soft-hearted as a chicken. His name must positively not be inquired, she said; to be thankful to him was to depart, asking no questions.

"And with a dart in the bosom from those eyes—those eyes!" cried Jack, shaking his head at the landlady's resistless charms.

"I hope you was not one of the gentlemen who came and disturbed us last night, Sir?" she turned on him sharply.

Jack dallied with the imputation, but denied his guilt.

"No; it wasn't your voice," continued the landlady. "A parcel of young puppies calling themselves gentlemen! I know him. It's that young Mr. Laxley: and he the nephew of a Bishop, and one of the Honourables! and then the poor gals get the blame. I call it a shame, I do. There's that poor young creature up-stairs—somebody's victim she is: and nobody's to suffer but herself, the little fool!"

"Yes," said Raikes. "Ah! we regret these things in after life!" and he looked as if he had many gentlemanly burdens of the kind on his conscience.

"It's a wonder, to my mind," remarked the landlady, when she had placidly surveyed Mr. Raikes, "how young gals can let some of you men-folk mislead 'em."

She turned from him huffily, and addressed Evan:

"The old gentleman is gone, sir. He slept on a chair, breakfasted, and was off before eight. He left word, as the child was born on his birthright, he'd provide for it, and pay the mother's bill, unless you claimed the right. I'm afraid he suspected—what I never, never-no! but by what I've seen of you—never will believe. For you, I'd say, must be a gentleman, whatever your company. She asks one favour of you, sir:—for you to go and let her speak to you once before you go away for good. She's asleep now, and mustn't be disturbed. Will you do it, by-and-by? Please to comfort the poor creature, sir."

Evan consented. I am afraid also it was the landlady's flattering speech made him, without reckoning his means, add that the young mother and her child must be considered under his care, and their expenses charged to him. The landlady was obliged to think him a wealthy as well as a noble youth, and admiringly curtsied.

Mr. John Raikes and Mr. Evan Harrington then strolled into the air, and through a long courtyard, with brewhouse and dairy on each side, and a pleasant smell of baking bread, and dogs winking in the sun, cats at the corners of doors, satisfied with life, and turkeys parading, and fowls, strutting cocks, that overset the dignity of Mr. Raikes by awakening his imitative propensities. Certain white-capped women, who were washing in a tub, laughed, and one observed: "He's for all the world like the little bantam cock stickin' 'self up in a crow against the Spaniar'." And this, and the landlady's marked deference to Evan, induced Mr. Raikes contemptuously to glance at our national blindness to the true diamond, and worship of the mere plumes in which a person is dressed.

They passed a pretty flower-garden, and entering a smooth-shorn meadow, beheld the downs beautifully clear under sunlight and slowly-sailing images of cloud. At the foot of the downs, on a plain of grass, stood a white booth topped by a flag, which signalled that on that spot Fallowfield and Beckley were contending.

"A singular old gentleman! A very singular old gentleman, that!" Raikes observed, following an idea that had been occupying him. "We did wrong to miss him. We ought to have waylaid him in the morning. Never miss a chance, Harrington."

"What chance?" Evan inquired.

"Those old gentlemen are very odd," Jack pursued, "very strange. He wouldn't have judged me by my attire. Admetus' flocks I guard, yet am a God! Dress is nothing to those old cocks. He's an eccentric. I know it; I can see it. He's a corrective of Cudford, who is abhorrent to my soul. To give you an instance, now, of what those old boys will do—I remember my father taking me, when I was quite a youngster, to a tavern he frequented, and we met one night just such an old fellow as this; and the waiter told us afterwards that he noticed me particularly. He thought me a very remarkable boy—predicted great things. For some reason or other my father never took me there again. I remember our having a Welsh rarebit there for supper, and when the waiter last night mentioned a rarebit, 'gad he started up before me. I gave chase into my early youth. However, my father never took me to meet the old fellow again. I believe it lost me a fortune."

Evan's thoughts were leaping to the cricket-field, or he would have condoled with Mr. Raikes for a loss that evidently afflicted him still.

Now, it must be told that the lady's-maid of Mrs. Andrew Cogglesby, borrowed temporarily by the Countess de Saldar for service at Beckley Court, had slept in charge of the Countess's boxes at the Green Dragon: the Countess having told her, with the candour of high-born dames to their attendants, that it would save expense; and that, besides, Admiral Combleman, whom she was going to see, or Sir Perkins Ripley (her father's old friend), whom she should visit if Admiral Combleman was not at his mansion—both were likely to have full houses, and she could not take them by storm. An arrangement which left her upwards of twelve hours' liberty, seemed highly proper to Maria Conning, this lady's-maid, a very demure young person. She was at her bed-room window, as Evan passed up the courtyard of the inn, and recognized him immediately. "Can it be him they mean that's the low tradesman?" was Maria's mysterious exclamation. She examined the pair, and added: "Oh, no. It must be the tall one they mistook for the small one. But Mr. Harrington ought not to demean himself by keeping company with such, and my lady should know of it."

My lady, alighting from the Lymport coach, did know of it, within a few minutes after Evan had quitted the Green Dragon, and turned pale, as high-born dames naturally do when they hear of a relative's disregard of the company he keeps.

"A tailor, my lady!" said scornful Maria; and the Countess jumped and complained of a pin.

"How did you hear of this, Conning?" she presently asked with composure.

"Oh, my lady, he was tipsy last night, and kept swearing out loud he was a gentleman."

"Tipsy!" the Countess murmured in terror. She had heard of inaccessible truths brought to light by the magic wand of alcohol. Was Evan intoxicated, and his dreadful secret unlocked last night?

"And who may have told you of this, Conning?" she asked.

Maria plunged into one of the boxes, and was understood to say that nobody in particular had told her, but that among other flying matters it had come to her ears.

"My brother is Charity itself," sighed the Countess. "He welcomes high or low."

"Yes, but, my lady, a tailor!" Maria repeated, and the Countess, agreeing with her scorn as she did, could have killed her. At least she would have liked to run a bodkin into her, and make her scream. In her position she could not always be Charity itself: nor is this the required character for a high-born dame: so she rarely affected it.

"Order a fly: discover the direction Mr. Harrington has taken; spare me further remarks," she said; and Maria humbly flitted from her presence.

When she was gone, the Countess covered her face with her hands. "Even this creature would despise us!" she exclaimed.

The young lady encountered by Mr. Raikes on the road to Fallowfield, was wrong in saying that Beckley would be seen out before the shades of evening caught up the ball. Not one, but two men of Beckley—the last two—carried out their bats, cheered handsomely by both parties. The wickets pitched in the morning, they carried them in again, and plaudits renewed proved that their fame had not slumbered. To stand before a field, thoroughly aware that every successful stroke you make is adding to the hoards of applause in store for you is a joy to your friends, an exasperation to your foes; I call this an exciting situation, and one as proud as a man may desire. Then, again, the two last men of an eleven are twins: they hold one life between them; so that he who dies extinguishes the other. Your faculties are stirred to their depths. You become engaged in the noblest of rivalries: in defending your own, you fight for your comrade's existence. You are assured that the dread of shame, if not emulation, is making him equally wary and alert.

Behold, then, the two bold men of Beckley fighting to preserve one life. Under the shadow of the downs they stand, beneath a glorious day, and before a gallant company. For there are ladies in carriages here, there are cavaliers; good county names may be pointed out. The sons of first-rate families are in the two elevens, mingled with the yeomen and whoever can best do the business. Fallowfield and Beckley, without regard to rank, have drawn upon their muscle and science. One of the bold men of Beckley at the wickets is Nick Frim, son of the gamekeeper at Beckley Court; the other is young Tom Copping, son of Squire Copping, of Dox Hall, in the parish of Beckley. Last year, you must know, Fallowfield beat. That is why Nick Frim, a renowned out-hitter, good to finish a score brilliantly with a pair of threes, has taken to blocking, and Mr. Tom cuts with caution, though he loves to steal his runs, and is usually dismissed by his remarkable cunning.

The field was ringing at a stroke of Nick Frim's, who had lashed out in his old familiar style at last, and the heavens heard of it, when Evan came into the circle of spectators. Nick and Tom were stretching from post to post, might and main. A splendid four was scored. The field took breath with the heroes; and presume not to doubt that heroes they are. It is good to win glory for your country; it is also good to win glory for your village. A Member of Parliament, Sir George Lowton, notes this emphatically, from the statesman's eminence, to a group of gentlemen on horseback round a carriage wherein a couple of fair ladies reclined.

"They didn't shout more at the news of the Battle of Waterloo. Now this is our peculiarity, this absence of extreme centralization. It must be encouraged. Local jealousies, local rivalries, local triumphs—these are the strength of the kingdom."

"If you mean to say that cricket's a ——" the old squire speaking (Squire Uplift of Fallowfield) remembered the saving presences, and coughed—"good thing, I'm one with ye, Sir George. Encouraged, egad! They don't want much of that here. Give some of your lean London straws a strip o' clean grass and a bit o' liberty, and you'll do 'em a service."

"What a beautiful hit!" exclaimed one of the ladies, languidly watching the ascent of the ball.

"Beautiful, d' ye call it?" muttered the squire.

The ball, indeed, was dropping straight into the hands of the long-hit-off. Instantly a thunder rolled. But it was Beckley that took the joyful treble—Fallowfield the deeply-cursing bass. The long-hit-off, he who never was known to miss a catch—butter-fingered beast!—he has let the ball slip through his fingers.

Are there Gods in the air? Fred Linnington, the unfortunate of Fallowfield, with a whole year of unhappy recollection haunting him in prospect, ere he can retrieve his character—Fred, if he does not accuse the powers of the sky, protests that he cannot understand it, which means the same.

Fallowfield's defeat—should such be the result of the contest—he knows now will be laid at his door. Five men who have bowled at the indomitable Beckleyans think the same. Albeit they are Britons, it abashes them. They are not the men they were. Their bowling is as the bowling of babies; and see! Nick, who gave the catch, and pretends he did it out of commiseration for Fallowfield, the ball has flown from his bat sheer over the booth. If they don't add six to the score, it will be the fault of their legs. But no: they rest content with a fiver and cherish their wind.

Yet more they mean to do, Success does not turn the heads of these Britons, as it would of your frivolous foreigners.

And now small boys (who represent the Press here) spread out from the marking-booth, announcing foremost, and in larger type, as it were, quite in Press style, their opinion—which is, that Fallowfield will get a jolly good hiding; and vociferating that Beckley is seventy-nine ahead, and that Nick Frim, the favourite of the field, has scored fifty-one to his own cheek. The boys are boys of both villages: but they are British boys—they adore prowess. The Fallowfield boys wish that Nick Frim would come and live on their side; the boys of Beckley rejoice in possessing him. Nick is the wicketkeeper of the Beckley eleven; long-limbed, wiry, keen of eye. His fault as a batsman is, that he will be a slashing hitter. He is too sensible of the joys of a grand spanking hit. A short life and a merry one, has hitherto been his motto.

But there were reasons for Nick's rare display of skill. That woman may have the credit due to her (and, as there never was a contest of which she did not sit at the springs, so is she the source of all superhuman efforts exhibited by men), be it told that Polly Wheedle is on the field; Polly, one of the upper housemaids of Beckley Court; Polly, eagerly courted by Fred Linnington, humbly desired by Nick Frim—a pert and blooming maiden—who, while her suitors combat hotly for an undivided smile, improves her holiday by instilling similar unselfish aspirations into the breasts of others.

Between his enjoyment of society and the melancholy it engendered in his mind by reflecting on him the age and decrepitude of his hat, Mr. John Raikes was doubtful of his happiness for some time. But as his taste for happiness was sharp, he, with a great instinct amounting almost to genius in its pursuit, resolved to extinguish his suspicion by acting the perfectly happy man. To do this, it was necessary that he should have listeners: Evan was not enough, and was besides unsympathetic; he had not responded to Jack's cordial assurances of his friendship "in spite of anything," uttered before they came into the field.

Heat and lustre were now poured from the sky, on whose soft blue a fleet of clouds sailed heavily. Nick Frim was very wonderful, no doubt. He deserved that the Gods should recline on those gold-edged cushions above, and lean over to observe him. Nevertheless, the ladies were beginning to ask when Nick Frim would be out. The small boys alone preserved their enthusiasm for Nick. As usual, the men took a middle position. Theirs was the pleasure of critics, which, being founded on the judgement, lasts long, and is without disappointment at the close. It was sufficient that the ladies should lend the inspiration of their bonnets to this fine match. Their presence on the field is another beautiful instance of the generous yielding of the sex simply to grace our amusement, and their acute perception of the part they have to play.

Mr. Raikes was rather shy of them at first. But his acting rarely failing to deceive himself, he began to feel himself the perfectly happy man he impersonated, and where there were ladies he went, and talked of days when he had creditably handled a bat, and of a renown in the annals of Cricket cut short by mysterious calamity. The foolish fellow did not know that they care not a straw for cricketing fame. His gaiety presently forsook him as quickly as it had come. Instead of remonstrating at Evan's restlessness, it was he who now dragged Evan from spot to spot. He spoke low and nervously.

"We're watched!"

There was indeed a man lurking near and moving as they moved, with a speculative air. Writs were out against Raikes. He slipped from his friend, saying:

"Never mind me. That old amphitryon's birthday hangs on till the meridian; you understand. His table invites. He is not unlikely to enjoy my conversation. What mayn't that lead to? Seek me there."

Evan strolled on, relieved by the voluntary departure of the weariful funny friend he would not shake off, but could not well link with.

A long success is better when seen at a distance of time, and Nick Frim was beginning to suffer from the monotony of his luck. Fallowfield could do nothing with him. He no longer blocked. He lashed out at every ball, and far flew every ball that was bowled. The critics saw, in this return to his old practices, promise of Nick's approaching extinction. The ladies were growing hot and weary. The little boys gasped on the grass, but like cunning circulators of excitement, spread a report to keep it up, that Nick, on going to his wickets the previous day, had sworn an oath that he would not lay down his bat till he had scored a hundred.

So they had still matter to agitate their youthful breasts, and Nick's gradual building up of tens, and prophecies and speculations as to his chances of completing the hundred, were still vehemently confided to the field, amid a general mopping of faces.

Evan did become aware that a man was following him. The man had not the look of a dreaded official. His countenance was sun-burnt and open, and he was dressed in a countryman's holiday suit. When Evan met his eyes, they showed perplexity. Evan felt he was being examined from head to heel, but by one unaccustomed to his part, and without the courage to decide what he ought consequently to do while a doubt remained, though his inspection was verging towards a certainty in his mind.

At last, somewhat annoyed that the man should continue to dog him wherever he moved, he turned on him and asked him what he wanted?

"Be you a Muster Eav'n Harrington, Esquire?" the man drawled out in the rustic music of inquiry.

"That is my name," said Evan.

"Ay," returned the man, "it's somebody lookin' like a lord, and has a small friend wi' shockin' old hat, and I see ye come out o' the Green Drag'n this mornin'—I don't reck'n there's e'er a mistaak, but I likes to make cock sure. Be you been to Poortigal, sir?"

"Yes," answered Evan, "I have been to Poortigal."

"What's the name o' the capital o' Portugal, sir?" The man looked immensely shrewd, and nodding his consent at the laughing reply, added:

"And there you was born, sir? You'll excuse my boldness, but I only does what's necessary."

Evan said he was not born there.

"No, not born there. That's good. Now, sir, did you happen to be born anywheres within smell o' salt water?"

"Yes," answered Evan, "I was born by the sea."

"Not far beyond fifty mile from Fall'field here, sir?"

"Something less."

"All right. Now I'm cock sure," said the man. "Now, if you'll have the kindness just to oblige me by—" he sped the words and the instrument jointly at Evan, "—takin' that there letter, I'll say good-bye, sir, and my work's done for the day."

Saying which, he left Evan with the letter in his hands. Evan turned it over curiously. It was addressed to "Evan Harrington, Esquire, T—— of Lymport."

A voice paralyzed his fingers: the clear ringing voice of a young horsewoman, accompanied by a little maid on a pony, who galloped up to the carriage upon which Squire Uplift, Sir George Lowton, Hamilton Jocelyn, and other cavaliers, were in attendance.

"Here I am at last, and Beckley's in still! How d' ye do, Lady Racial? How d' ye do, Sir George. How d' ye do, everybody. Your servant, Squire!

We shall beat you. Harry says we shall soon be a hundred a-head of you. Fancy those boys! they would sleep at Fallowfield last night. How I wish you had made a bet with me, Squire."

"Well, my lass, it's not too late," said the Squire, detaining her hand.

"Oh, but it wouldn't be fair now. And I'm not going to be kissed on the field, if you please, Squire. Here, Dorry will do instead. Dorry! come and be kissed by the Squire."

It was Rose, living and glowing; Rose, who was the brilliant young Amazon, smoothing the neck of a mettlesome gray cob. Evan's heart bounded up to her, but his limbs were motionless.

The Squire caught her smaller companion in his arms, and sounded a kiss upon both her cheeks; then settled her in the saddle, and she went to answer some questions of the ladies. She had the same lively eyes as Rose; quick saucy lips, red, and open for prattle. Rolls of auburn hair fell down her back, for being a child she was allowed privileges. To talk as her thoughts came, as well as to wear her hair as it grew, was a special privilege of this young person, on horseback or elsewhere.

"Now, I know what you want to ask me, Aunt Shorne. Isn't it about my Papa? He's not come, and he won't be able to come for a week.—Glad to be with Cousin Rosey? I should think I am! She's the nicest girl I ever could suppose. She isn't a bit spoiled by Portugal; only browned; and she doesn't care for that; no more do I. I rather like the sun when it doesn't freckle you. I can't bear freckles, and I don't believe in milk for them. People who have them are such a figure. Drummond Forth has them, but he's a man, and it doesn't matter for a man to have freckles. How's my uncle Mel? Oh, he's quite well. I mean he has the gout in one of his fingers, and it's swollen so, it's just like a great fat fir cone! He can't write a bit, and rests his hand on a table. He wants to have me made to write with my left hand as well as my right. As if I was ever going to have the gout in one of my fingers!"

Sir George Lowton observed to Hamilton Jocelyn, that Melville must take to his tongue now.

"I fancy he will," said Hamilton. "My father won't give up his nominee; so I fancy he'll try Fallowfield. Of course, we go in for the agricultural interest; but there's a cantankerous old ruffian down here—a brewer, or something—he's got half the votes at his bidding. We shall see."

"Dorothy, my dear child, are you not tired?" said Lady Racial. "You are very hot."

"Yes, that's because Rose would tear along the road to get here in time, after we had left those tiresome Copping people, where she had to make a call. 'What a slow little beast your pony is, Dorry!'—she said that at least twenty times."

"Oh, you naughty puss!" cried Rose. "Wasn't it, 'Rosey, Rosey, I'm sure we shall be too late, and shan't see a thing: do come along as hard as you can'?"

"I'm sure it was not," Miss Dorothy retorted, with the large eyes of innocence. "You said you wanted to see Nick Frim keeping the wicket, and Ferdinand Laxley bowl. And, oh! you know something you said about Drummond Forth."

"Now, shall I tell upon you?" said Rose.

"No, don't!" hastily replied the little woman, blushing. And the cavaliers laughed out, and the ladies smiled, and Dorothy added: "It isn't much, after all."

"Then, come; let's have it, or I shall be jealous," said the Squire.

"Shall I tell?" Rose asked slily.

"It's unfair to betray one of your sex, Rose," remarked the sweetly-smiling lady.

"Yes, Lady Racial—mayn't a woman have secrets?" Dorothy put it with great natural earnestness, and they all laughed aloud. "But I know a secret of Rosey's," continued Miss Dorothy, "and if she tells upon me, I shall tell upon her."

"They're out!" cried Rose, pointing her whip at the wickets. "Good night to Beckley! Tom Copping's run out."

Questions as to how it was done passed from mouth to mouth. Questions as to whether it was fair sprang from Tom's friends, and that a doubt existed was certain: the whole field was seen converging toward the two umpires.

Farmer Broadmead for Fallowfield, Master Nat Hodges for Beckley.

It really is a mercy there's some change in the game," said Mrs. Shorne, waving her parasol. "It's a charming game, but it wants variety a little. When do you return, Rose?"

"Not for some time," said Rose, primly. "I like variety very well, but I don't seek it by running away the moment I've come."

"No, but, my dear," Mrs. Shorne negligently fanned her face, "you will have to come with us, I fear, when we go. Your uncle accompanies us. I really think the Squire will, too; and Mr. Forth is no chaperon. Even you understand that."

"Oh, I can get an old man—don't be afraid, said Rose. "Or must I have an old woman, aunt?"

The lady raised her eyelids slowly on Rose, and thought: "If you were soundly whipped, my little madam, what a good thing it would be for you." And that good thing Mrs. Shorne was willing to do for Rose. She turned aside, and received the salute of an unmistakable curate on foot.

"Ah, Mr. Parsley, you lend your countenance to the game, then?"

The curate observed that sound Churchmen unanimously supported the game.

"Bravo!" cried Rose. "How I like to hear you talk like that, Mr. Parsley. I didn't think you had so much sense. You and I will have a game together—single wicket. We must play for something—what shall it be?"

"Oh—for nothing," the curate vacuously remarked.

"That's for love, you rogue!" exclaimed the Squire. "Come, come, none o' that, sir—ha! ha!"

"Oh, very well; we'll play for love," said Rose.

"And I'll hold the stakes, my dear—eh?"

"You dear old naughty Squire!—what do you mean?"

Rose laughed. But she had all the men surrounding her, and Mrs. Shorne talked of departing.

Why did not Evan bravely march away? Why, he asked himself, had he come on this cricket-field to be made thus miserable? What right had such as he to look on Rose? Consider, however, the young man's excuses. He could not possibly imagine that a damsel who rode one day to a match, would return on the following day to see it finished: or absolutely know that unseen damsel to be Rose Jocelyn. And if he waited, it was only to hear her sweet voice once again, and go for ever. As far as he could fathom his hopes, they were that Rose would not see him: but the hopes of youth are deep.

Just then a toddling small rustic stopped in front of Evan, and set up a howl for his "fayther." Evan lifted him high to look over people's heads, and discover his wandering parent. The urchin, when he had settled to his novel position, surveyed the field, and shouting, "Fayther, fayther! here I bes on top of a gentleman!" made lusty signs, which attracted not his father alone. Rose sang out, "Who can lend me a penny?" Instantly the curate and the squire had a race in their pockets. The curate was first, but Rose favoured the squire, took his money with a nod and a smile, and rode at the little lad, to whom she was saying: "Here, bonny boy, this will buy you—"

She stopped and coloured.

"Evan!"

The child descended rapidly to the ground.

A bow and a few murmured words replied to her.

"Isn't this just like you, my dear Evan? Shouldn't I know that whenever I met you, you would be doing something kind? How did you come here? You were on your way to Beckley!"

"To London," said Evan.

"To London! and not coming over to see me—us?"

Here the little fellow's father intervened to claim his offspring, and thank the lady and the gentleman: and, with his penny firmly grasped, he who had brought the lady and the gentleman together, was borne off a wealthy human creature.

Before much further could be said between them, the Countess de Saldar drove up.

"My dearest Rose!" and "My dear Countess!" and "Not Louisa, then?" and, "I am very glad to see you!" without attempting the endearing "Louisa"—passed.

The Countess de Saldar then admitted the presence of her brother.

"Think!" said Rose. "He talks of going on straight from here to London."

"That pretty pout will alone suffice to make him deviate, then," said the Countess, with her sweetest open slyness. "I am now on the point of accepting your most kind invitation. Our foreign habits allow us to visit thus early! He will come with me."

Evan tried to look firm, and speak as he was trying to look. Rose fell to entreaty, and from entreaty rose to command; and in both was utterly fascinating to the poor youth. Luxuriously—while he hesitated and dwelt on this and that faint objection—his spirit drank the delicious changes of her face. To have her face before him but one day seemed so rich a boon to deny himself, that he was beginning to wonder at his constancy in refusal; and now that she spoke to him so pressingly, devoting her guileless eyes to him alone, he forgot a certain envious feeling that had possessed him while she was rattling among the other males—a doubt whether she ever cast a thought on Mr. Evan Harrington.

"Yes; he will come," cried Rose; "and he shall ride home with me and my friend Drummond; and he shall have my groom's horse, if he doesn't mind. Bob can ride home in the cart with Polly, my maid; and he'll like that, because Polly's always good fun—when they're not in love with her. Then, of course, she torments them."

"Naturally," said the Countess.

Mr. Evan Harrington's final objection, based on his not having clothes, and so forth, was met by his foreseeing sister.

"I have your portmanteau packed, in with me, my dear brother; Conning has her feet on it. I divined that I should overtake you."

Evan felt he was in the toils. After a struggle or two he yielded; and, having yielded, did it with grace. In a moment, and with a power of self-compression equal to that of the adept Countess, he threw off his moodiness as easily as if it had been his Spanish mantle, and assumed a gaiety that made the Countess's eyes beam rapturously upon him, and was pleasing to Rose, apart from the lead in admiration the Countess had given her—not for the first time. We mortals, the best of us, may be silly sheep in our likes and dislikes: where there is no premeditated or instinctive antagonism, we can be led into warm acknowledgement of merits we have not sounded. This the Countess de Saldar knew right well.

Rose now intimated her wish to perform the ceremony of introduction between her aunt and uncle present, and the visitors to Beckley Court. The Countess smiled, and in the few paces that separated the two groups, whispered to her brother: "Miss Jocelyn, my dear."

The eye-glasses of the Beckley group were dropped with one accord. The ceremony was gone through. The softly-shadowed differences of a grand manner addressed to ladies, and to males, were exquisitely accomplished by the Countess de Saldar.

"Harrington? Harrington?" her quick ear caught on the mouth of Squire Uplift, scanning Evan.

Her accent was very foreign, as she said aloud: "We are entirely strangers to your game—your creecket. My brother and myself are scarcely English. Nothing save diplomacy are we adepts in!"

"You must be excessively dangerous, madam," said Sir George, hat in air.

"Even in that, I fear, we are babes and sucklings, and might take many a lesson from you. Will you instruct me in your creecket? What are they doing now? It seems very unintelligible—indistinct—is it not?"

Inasmuch as Farmer Broadmead and Master Nat Hodges were surrounded by a clamorous mob, shouting both sides of the case, as if the loudest and longest-winded were sure to wrest a favourable judgement from those two infallible authorities on the laws of cricket, the noble game was certainly in a state of indistinctness.

The squire came forward to explain, piteously entreated not to expect too much from a woman's inapprehensive wits, which he plainly promised (under eyes that had melted harder men) he would not. His forbearance and bucolic gallantry were needed, for he had the Countess's radiant full visage alone. Her senses were dancing in her right ear, which had heard the name of Lady Racial pronounced, and a voice respond to it from the carriage.

Into what a pit had she suddenly plunged! You ask why she did not drive away as fast as the horses would carry her, and fly the veiled head of Demogorgon obscuring valley and hill and the shining firmament, and threatening to glare destruction on her? You do not know an intriguer. She relinquishes the joys of life for the joys of intrigue. This is her element. The Countess did feel that the heavens were hard on her. She resolved none the less to fight her way to her object; for where so much had conspired to favour her—the decease of the generous Sir Abraham Harrington, of Torquay, and the invitation to Beckley Court—could she believe the heavens in league against her? Did she not nightly pray to them, in all humbleness of body, for the safe issue of her cherished schemes? And in this, how unlike she was to the rest of mankind! She thought so; she relied on her devout observances; they gave her sweet confidence, and the sense of being specially shielded even when specially menaced. Moreover, tell a woman to put back, when she is once clearly launched! Timid as she may be, her light bark bounds to meet the tempest. I speak of women who do launch: they are not numerous, but, to the wise, the minorities are the representatives.

"Indeed, it is an intricate game!" said the Countess, at the conclusion of the squire's explanation, and leaned over to Mrs. Shorne to ask her if she thoroughly understood it.

"Yes, I suppose I do," was the reply; "it—rather than the amusement they find in it." This lady had recovered Mr. Parsley from Rose, but had only succeeded in making the curate unhappy, without satisfying herself.

The Countess gave her the shrug of secret sympathy.

"We must not say so," she observed aloud—most artlessly, and fixed the squire with a bewitching smile, under which her heart beat thickly. As her eyes travelled from Mrs. Shorne to the squire, she had marked Lady Racial looking singularly at Evan, who was mounting the horse of Bob the groom.

"Fine young fellow, that," said the squire to Lady Racial, as Evan rode off with Rose.

"An extremely handsome, well-bred young man," she answered. Her eyes met the Countess's, and the Countess, after resting on their surface with an ephemeral pause, murmured: "I must not praise my brother," and smiled a smile which was meant to mean: "I think with you, and thank you, and love you for admiring him."

Had Lady Racial joined the smile and spoken with animation afterwards, the Countess would have shuddered and had chills of dread. As it was, she was passably content. Lady Racial slightly dimpled her cheek, for courtesy's sake, and then looked gravely on the ground. This was no promise; it was even an indication (as the Countess read her), of something beyond suspicion in the lady's mind; but it was a sign of delicacy, and a sign that her feelings had been touched, from which a truce might be reckoned on, and no betrayal feared.

She heard it said that the match was for honour and glory. A match of two days' duration under a broiling sun, all for honour and glory! Was it not enough to make her despise the games of men? For something better she played. Her game was for one hundred thousand pounds, the happiness of her brother, and the concealment of a horror. To win a game like that was worth the trouble. Whether she would have continued her efforts, had she known that the name of Evan Harrington was then blazing on a shop-front in Lymport, I cannot tell. The possessor of the name was in love, and did not reflect.

Smiling adieu to the ladies, bowing to the gentlemen, and apprehending all the homage they would pour out to her condescending beauty when she had left them, the Countess's graceful hand gave the signal for Beckley.

She stopped the coachman ere the wheels had rolled off the muffling turf, to enjoy one glimpse of Evan and Rose riding together, with the little maid on her pony in the rear. How suitable they seemed! how happy! She had brought them together after many difficulties—might it not be? It was surely a thing to be hoped for!

Rose, galloping freshly, was saying to Evan: "Why did you cut off your moustache?"

He, neck and neck with her, replied: "You complained of it in Portugal."

And she: "Portugal's old times now to me—and I always love old times. I'm sorry! And, oh, Evan! did you really do it for me?"

And really, just then, flying through the air, close to the darling of his heart, he had not the courage to spoil that delicious question, but dallying with the lie, he looked in her eyes lingeringly.

This picture the Countess contemplated. Close to her carriage two young gentlemen-cricketers were strolling, while Fallowfield gained breath to decide which men to send in first to the wickets.

One of these stood suddenly on tiptoe, and pointing to the pair on horseback, cried, with the vivacity of astonishment:

"Look there! do you see that? What the deuce is little Rosey doing with the tailor-fellow?"

The Countess, though her cheeks were blanched, gazed calmly in Demogorgon's face, took a mental impression of the speaker, and again signalled for Beckley.